C0-DAO-558

# In Search
# of Valor

## Gary Corbin

This book is a work of fiction. Names,
characters, businesses, incidents, and dialogue
are either drawn from the author's imagination or
are used fictitiously, and are not to be construed
as real. Any resemblance to actual events or
persons, living or dead, is entirely coincidental.

Copyright © 2020 Gary Corbin
Double Diamond Publishing, Camas, WA
All rights reserved.
ISBN: 978-1-7346152-0-3

*To all of the people
who have read each book I've written.
Your faith in me and your unflagging  support
keeps me writing.*

# Chapter One

The short, squat man shaded his eyes, as much to hide his face as to shield his vision against the intense late-summer sun. "Built like a fireplug, sweats like a pig," his football coach used to say. Mostly to get under his skin, but also to make an excuse for not letting him play quarterback. Never mind that he had the best arm on the team and could read defenses better than anyone. That he could outrun all but the fleetest of wide receivers and running backs, and every last defensive lineman who lumbered after him in parks-and-rec league. That he'd broken records for touchdowns and passing yardage in junior high ball. And—

Dammit! Focus! He cursed himself and shook his head to force the distracting thoughts away. Look for the girl. Ensure she's a safe distance from Ground Zero. And that she didn't return to her car and drive to where her kid played under adult supervision...for now.

He smiled. Such a great plan. If he didn't have such an important job to do at the moment, he'd pat himself on the back, literally. Something his coach would never do.

Movement caught his eye to the left. A tall, curvy woman with light brown skin and thick black curls emerged from the parking structure. Even wearing those stupid oversized sunglasses, he recognized her. The bitch. He'd never forget that face. That condescending stare, telling him he wasn't good enough for her.

She'd regret that decision. He'd make sure of it.

He watched her walk for a moment, striding toward the center of campus, checking her cell phone. Oblivious. Unsuspecting.

Perfect.

He tapped a message into the burner phone in his hand. "Move. Now." Hit Send. Then he walked in the opposite direction from her, tossing the burner into a garbage can on the way to his car, never looking back.

# Chapter Two

Valorie Dawes averted her hazel eyes from the intense morning sun, an unseasonably warm mid-September day on the campus of the University of Connecticut. She'd dressed for the heat: shorts, running shoes, and a "Property of UConn Huskies" t-shirt. Nevertheless, sweat dripped down her back, soaking not only her skin, but also the sturdy backpack holding her books and laptop. She brushed damp, light-brown hair away from her face and stretched her wiry, five-foot-six frame onto her tiptoes to see over the heads of a few oncoming upperclassmen. Still no sign of her.

She checked the time on her cell phone. She'd arrived at 9:25, five minutes early, but that was fifteen minutes ago. Maybe she'd gotten the location wrong.

Val searched the busy sidewalks, crowded with students hurrying to their next air-conditioned classroom. Still no sign of Rhonda LeMieux's tall, curvy frame. Despite having moved to the mainland in her teens, Rhonda continued to operate on what she called "Jamaica time." Her habitual lateness had made her a favorite whipping post of their cantankerous professor of Criminology, Warren Hirsch. Doubts crept into Val's mind once again over her choice of a research partner for the Crim 101 term paper, the first class in her chosen major.

She scolded herself a moment later. Rhonda had mentioned when they'd first met that she had a daughter, and as a young single mother, she worried constantly about the girl's well-being. No doubt something had come up with the girl's care, and—

"Well, well, what have we here?" said a familiar male voice. She turned toward the glass doors of the Student Union entrance. A thin-shouldered, blond-haired man wearing khaki shorts, a Polo shirt, and deck shoes stared back at her behind expensive Oakley sunglasses. He uncrossed his arms and pushed off of his shaded perch, ambling toward her with a silly grin on his face. "If it isn't the famous Val Dawes, all by her lonesome."

"Hoping to stay that way, too, Robb," she said, sighing. If anyone on the UConn campus represented privilege and arrogance, it was Robbin J. McFarland. "Esquire," as he'd emphasized when introducing himself on the first day of classes a few weeks before. She'd joined the few women and most of the men in the classroom in a group eye roll, but Robb remained oblivious.

"What are you waiting for, the press to show up and interview you *again*?" he said with a sneer. "Oh, right. *That* hasn't happened yet. That must be *absolutely* killing you, am I right, *Val*?"

"My name's Valorie," she said, then smirked. "Only my friends call me Val."

"Well, *excuu-uuse* me." Robb stepped closer to

her. "I wouldn't want to presume. I only wondered if you'd reconsidered my offer."

"Which one?" She eased away from him, squeamishness rising in her abdomen, and scanned the sidewalks again for Rhonda. "The four awkward invitations to go out with you, or the even more absurd notion of partnering with you on the Criminology paper?"

"Oh, so you do remember." He smiled, which made his face resemble a snake's, or a fully shaved weasel. He wiped sweat from his brow with a handkerchief and edged closer. His six-foot-plus frame towered over her. "Well, I thought we could kill two birds with one stone and discuss our project over dinner tonight." He reached out to touch her. Val batted it away, hard.

"Ow!" he said, rubbing his arm. "Geez Louise, Dawes. Such a slender little thing, but you sure pack a punch."

"Sorry," she said, not sounding sorry. "Martial-arts reflex. Happens every time someone misunderstands the word 'no.' Now, if you'll excuse me, I think I see my real research partner."

Sure enough, a tall, dark-haired woman sashayed up the walk with an enviable air of confidence. She appeared to be in her early 20s, with smooth, light-brown skin and a toothy smile. A bright yellow sundress hugged her curvy figure, and three-inch heels brought her eyes almost even with Robb's. Unlike Val and Robb, Rhonda seemed unaffected by the late August heat.

"Is this boy bothering you?" she asked in her island lilt. "You let me know, and I'll have my Jamaican boyfriends take care of him, eh?"

Robb blanched, edging away as Rhonda

approached. "Miss Dawes and I were just
discussing the potential of teaming up on—"

"*Ms.* Dawes and I," Rhonda said, her eyes
hardening, "are already a team. No room for you,
boyo."

"Oh, really?" Robb said. "And what do you bring
to the table, *Miz LeMoose*?"

"De name's LeMieux. That means, de best." Her
accent became more pronounced—intentional, Val
guessed. Rhonda's grin widened as she went on.
"And I live up to my name. Now go play on yo
sailboat, or whatever you do in Martha's Vineyard."
*Maw-taw's* Vin-*yawd*, to Val's ears.

"Narra-*gan*-set, please," Robb scoffed. "For
Gawd's sake. Don't lump me in with the freaking
Kennedys." He turned away, his nose high in the
air, and strode off, muttering and shaking his head
in disgust.

Val expelled a loud breath and glanced at
Rhonda. "What a character," she said.

"Get used to it, my friend," Rhonda said. "These
rich UConn boys think themselves to be king. And
we are their pawns, no?"

"Not in my world," Val said. "So, are we a team
for real, then? We have to confirm with Dr. Hirsch
by Thursday afternoon."

"It would be my honor to partner with the niece
of the great Valentin Dawes," Rhonda said, tugging
her toward the building's entrance.

Val jerked to a stop, forcing Rhonda to halt her
progress as well. "None of that, okay?" Val said.
"Yeah, my uncle died a hero, and he means much
more to me than anyone will ever know. But I'm
not trading on his fame, and I don't expect you to,
either."

Rhonda hung her head and took a deep breath. "I'm sorry, Valorie. I meant it as a joke, only. Forgive my bad taste."

Val sighed. She envied Rhonda's unpretentious, laid-back style, one that contrasted so much from hers. She needed to learn how to be like that, somehow. "Of course. Apology accepted. So, why don't we get a cup of coffee and plan our project? I'll buy."

Rhonda grinned and extended her hand. "You got it, partner!"

\*\*\*

Ten minutes later, Val and Rhonda squeezed into adjacent seats at a tiny table in the crowded Student Union café. "I insist," Val said when Rhonda protested Val paying for their coffee. "I offered. Besides, don't you have a baby to feed?"

Rhonda laughed, a sound Val found infectious and charming. "Jada is only eighteen months old. She hardly eats anything." She showed Val a photo of a curly-haired girl in a pink dress whose smile seemed a miniature carbon copy of Rhonda's.

Val's heart melted at the sight of the little girl. "That's the same age as my niece, Alison," she said. "I love that little imp so much! And what a pretty name!"

"I knew I liked you for a reason," Rhonda said, grinning. "It's Jamaican, like my father, and it means 'God's gift.' And she is, to me. In fact, she is part of the reason I was late this morning. I drove almost the whole way to her day care center before I remembered we were meeting today." She checked her watch, a cheap Rolex knock-off. "I need to pick her up at day care in a half hour, so we'd better work fast. What topic should we choose?"

They opened their laptops and discussed the approved topics listed on Professor Hirsch's faculty page. "I like 'Women in Crime: Victims and Perpetrators,' but is that too predictable for us?" Val said.

"Maybe," Rhonda said. "What about 'The Rise of Hate Crimes' or 'Police Use of Force'? Same problem?"

"Those sound great to me—I love doing statistical research," Val said. "But what about you? As a future social worker, maybe we should choose a topic focused on families. 'Intergenerational Recidivism,' maybe, or the 'The Contributions of Poverty and Class to Urban Crime.' Are those better?"

Rhonda frowned. "Those don't sound like good fits for a future policewoman."

Val waved her off. "They're all relevant. Besides, I'm not a hundred percent decided on my major," she said. "You know, I've always thought I'd become a cop, since I was a kid. But over the last few months I've had second thoughts. I might be happier doing social work,too—helping troubled families in a more constructive way, before they get swept up by crime—as victims or perpetrators.. Locking them up after they commit crimes seems kind of a negative approach."

"If you grew up like I did, you'd definitely look at cops as a negative approach," Rhonda said. "My brother spent a week in jail for a crime he didn't commit. 'Mistaken identity,' they said. Yeah, it was a mistake all right. They arrested him for being young and black."

"That's terrible," Val said. "To be honest, though, my focus would be on supporting young women and girls—victims of abuse and such." She went quiet, her heart pounding.

*A silhouette filled the open doorway...the shadow of a large, overweight man, tufts of black and silver hair shining in the reflected light of the hallway. His heavy breathing filled her tiny bedroom with aromas of whiskey and sweat—*

Rhonda cocked her head. "Is that motivated by personal experience, or—"

"Just something I'm interested in," Val said in a rush of words, pushing the memory out of her mind. "We'd best not get sidetracked here. You said time was short, right?"

They kicked the options around and chose the "Women in Crime" topic. "If we don't, it'll be left to the Neanderthal men like Robb McFarland," Rhonda said. "I hate to think what that paper would look like."

After dividing up the initial research responsibilities, Rhonda gulped down her coffee. "I need to get to the day care center," she said. "It's over on the west side, just off campus. Can I give you a ride somewhere?"

"I'd love that," Val said. "The surplus store is out that way, and I need a more comfortable desk chair."

"I can drop you off after we pick up Jada," Rhonda said. "It'll give us a chance to chat more about the paper."

Instead, however, their conversation shifted to

more personal topics during the traffic-jammed ride across Storrs, a campus-focused village in the city of Mansfield. "Is your uncle the reason you want to go into law enforcement?" Rhonda asked.

"He definitely inspired me," Val said. "I saw how he made a difference in the community through police work. That's my real goal. I'm just not sure anymore if that's the right path for me. What about you? What motivated you to pursue social work?"

"When I first started, I wanted to make a difference in the community, like you," Rhonda said. "Now I just want to help women avoid the mistakes I made, try to keep them out of trouble." She fell silent a moment.

Val considered asking her to elaborate, then decided to steer the conversation toward less troubling topics. "You mentioned spending a year in college before you had Jada. Was that here, at UConn?"

Rhonda shook her head. "I had a full athletic scholarship to Yale," she said. "Volleyball and track. But I had to give it all up when I came back to Mansfield to take care of my mom."

"Wow!" Val said. "I have a partial scholarship— track and soccer. I didn't know women could even get a full ride for sports."

"Ah," Rhonda said. "That may be the only advantage of being a black woman in America. They assumed, correctly as it turns out, that I also had financial hardship. And finding female athletes of color with good grades is a very competitive market, it seems."

"That's awesome," Val said. "The scholarship, I mean. Will you be running track at UConn?"

Rhonda scoffed. "Not while raising a baby and

working full time. Besides, it's best if I keep a low profile. Rizzo, my baby's daddy, has threatened more than once to sue for custody...or just take matters into his own hands. I haven't even told him about returning to school. I'd rather he doesn't find out."

"He threatened to take the baby from you?" Val said, her voice hoarse. "That's outrageous!"

"You don't know the half of it," Rhonda said, pulling into the parking lot of the day care center. "A few months ago he saw me out to dinner with a man. He tried to pick a fight with the guy...until my date stood up. He was six-five and built like a steamroller. Rizzo suddenly realized that he was double-parked. I haven't seen him since."

Val laughed out loud. "You have a great way of putting things, Rhonda. Hey, is it okay if I come in with you? I'd love to meet Jada."

Rhonda enveloped Val in a bone-crushing hug. "Girl, I think I already love you like a sister," she said. "Come on! Shoot, I'm already five minutes late."

They hustled inside, and a mousy, brown-haired white woman with horn-rimmed glasses greeted them. "Are you picking up, or dropping off?" she asked with a saccharine smile.

Val and Rhonda exchanged puzzled glances. "You don't honestly think I'm her daughter?" Val said.

"Name?" the brown-haired woman responded without hesitation, fingers resting on her computer keyboard.

"LeMieux. My baby's name is Jada." Rhonda showed no surprise or impatience at the receptionist's cluelessness.

The receptionist smiled again and tapped at her keyboard. Puzzlement spread over her face. "Jada? J-A-Y-D-A?"

"No 'Y'," Rhonda said, sing-song. "LeMieux is L-E—"

"Ah, here she is," the receptionist said, but her smile evaporated. "There seems to be some confusion."

"What sort of confusion?" Rhonda said, her face forming a worried frown.

"She's already been picked up," the receptionist said. "About twenty minutes ago, by her grandmother."

"Her grandmother?" Rhonda's frown deepened. "That's impossible. Could you please check again?"

The receptionist clicked a few keys, frowning, but said nothing.

Val edged closer to Rhonda. "Are you sure your mother didn't come by and get her?" she asked.

Rhonda's eyes teared up, and she glanced at Val, her lips trembling. "I'm sure," she said. "My mother died six months ago." She paused a moment to regain her composure. "Her life insurance policy is paying my tuition."

"I'm sorry," the receptionist said. "We show that Jada left under the care of an approved guardian. The woman identified herself as Karina LeMieux."

Rhonda burst into tears and slumped into a chair, moaning. "He did it. That son of a bitch took her!"

Val drew a steadying breath and turned to the receptionist. "Miss, about the woman who took Jada. Did you get a signature, an I.D., anything?"

The woman pecked at her keyboard and stared at the screen. "I wasn't here—somebody else

checked Jada out," she said. "But her
grandmother is in our system as an approved
guardian."

"How is that possible? She's deceased, as
Rhonda just told you!" Val said.

Rhonda groaned. "I never got around to
updating my records here after Ma died," she said.
"Oh, my God. Oh, my God!"

Val leaned across the desk, her face inches from
the receptionist's. "You need to go check to make
sure that little girl isn't here," she said. "*Now!*"

The receptionist froze for a moment, then
disappeared through a door behind her.

# Chapter Three

Detective Tanisha Jordan parked her ten-year-old Dodge Charger in the "Reserved—Staff" spot in front of the day care center. Nice of them to leave it open for her, she joked to herself. She slapped a laminated green 8x10" card on her dash that read "Official Police Business," locked the vehicle, and took in her surroundings.

The facility occupied the western half of a small strip mall on a busy highway a mile from the UConn campus. The rest of the complex housed a Chinese restaurant, a convenience store, and a nail salon. Security cameras mounted on the fascia boards monitored the comings and goings, she guessed, of the whole building. She'd check their footage after interviewing the day care staff.

She scanned the surrounding area. An apartment complex towered above a thick stand of trees to the left. A series of 1950s-era single-family homes and duplexes lined the street to the right. A similar array of buildings dotted the other side of the highway. Lots of folks might have seen whoever took the child. But would they have suspected foul play of an adult carrying a child from day care to their car? Probably not.

Unless the perp looked like Tanisha. As in, black, first off. Whether or not they admitted it, most of lily-white Mansfield, Connecticut took immediate distrust to people of color. Especially if, like her, said child-carrying African American was not a female in prime child-bearing age. Few thirty-seven-year-old women met that description.

Still. Those buildings contained possible witnesses—leads to help solve the case.

And speed was of the essence in a true abduction case. The perps would move the child out of the area within a day or two. Or—she shuddered—much worse things could happen.

Jordan took a deep breath. Chill, girl. Don't jump to conclusions. This case would probably amount to a minor annoyance in the scheme of things. Most child abductions turned out to be false alarms. Often an angry ex-spouse picked the kid up out of turn to annoy their estranged ex. Other times, a grandparent or other relative did and failed to notify the parent. So this whole episode would waste a ton of her precious time she could better spend tracking down real perps. Plus it would probably put her in the middle of nasty family arguments she'd much rather avoid.

She entered the facility, and out of habit, drew herself up straight for maximum height. No one would call her athletic, 5'7" frame short, but height implied authority, especially among cops. She flashed her badge to the receptionist, a petite white woman with brown hair. "Detective Jordan, responding to a complaint—"

"Yes, right this way, Detective." The receptionist jumped out of her chair and led Jordan down a narrow hallway. She showed her into a small meeting room dominated by a long wooden table and a half-dozen chairs. Two young women—one black, the other white—sat along one edge of the table. She guessed them to be students, and for the older black one to be the complainant. A thin, gray-haired white woman, seated across from them, rose as Jordan entered. Distress lined the faces of all three.

"Welcome, Detective." The older woman shook Jordan's hand. "I'm Estelle Quarterman, the director of Little Husky Playpen. This is Rhonda LeMieux, Jada's mother."

The young black student nodded at her, but did not offer a handshake, instead wrapping her arms around herself, her face down. "Thank you for coming," she said, with a hint of a Jamaican accent.

Jordan turned to the young white gal, still seated next to Rhonda. "And you are...?"

The white gal startled from her chair, as if woken from a daydream. "Valorie Dawes," she said. "Friend of Rhonda's."

Jordan's mind whirled. Val Dawes? Jordan knew that name. "Any relation to—"

"He was my uncle." The girl half-smiled, half-grimaced, and sat back down. "It seems his reputation extends well outside of Clayton, then. You're the second person today who knew of him."

Jordan nodded. "When one of our own goes down, we all know. Besides, Clayton's not so far from here. Do you hope to become a police officer also, Miss Dawes?"

"Someday," Dawes said. "I'm just a first-year at UConn right now."

"Let's hope you inherited your uncle's genes for good detective work," Jordan said. "We might need it." Especially, she noted to herself, if her archery-obsessed partner continued to suffer with a "deer hunting season" flu, now in its third day. "Now, Mrs. LeMieux, let's start from the beginning. When did you discover your daughter missing?"

"It's Ms. LeMieux," Rhonda said through sniffles. "I never married. I discovered it when I got here to pick her up, about a half-hour ago."

"And you dropped her off at what time?" Jordan whipped out a notepad and pen.

"A few minutes before eight o'clock," Rhonda said. "I had an early class, then another at nine. Dammit, I should have come straight here after class!" She glared at Dawes for a moment, then turned away. Dawes reddened, but said nothing.

"Who picked the girl up, then?" Jordan asked Quarterman.

"Our records show that a woman claiming to be the child's grandmother—"

"My mother is dead!" LeMieux shouted. "I've told you this a hundred times!"

"Easy, easy," Jordan said. "Let's just get the facts here, okay? Now, Ms. Quarterman..."

"Call me Estelle, please. Now, as I was saying," Quarterman said, regaining her composure. "A woman calling herself Karina LeMieux checked Jada out around 9:50 a.m. She presented identification and signed our check-out form, and she was pre-approved by Ms. LeMieux to do so."

"I forgot to update my records," Rhonda said. Remorse choked her voice. "Nobody else knew this. This was an inside job. It had to be! Where's my baby? *Give me back my baby!*" She lunged across the table at Quarterman as if to grab her.

With surprising agility, the older woman somehow eluded Rhonda's grasp. Dawes wrapped

her arms around Rhonda's waist and guided her
back to her chair.

"I'd like to see your security footage for that
period," Jordan said to Quarterman. "Do you have
a physical description?"

Estelle nodded. "Average height, a little
overweight. African American, late forties to early
fifties—"

"My mother was white!" Rhonda shouted.
"Wasn't *that* in your files?"

Quarterman stared at her, stricken. "I,
uh...suppose not."

Jordan rubbed her temples. A headache
erupted in her frontal lobes. Crap. So much for this
being an easy family-miscommunication case. "I'll
want you to check this footage with me, Ms.
LeMieux. See if you recognize her. Is there anyone
else that meets her description? The child's other
grandmother, perhaps?"

"Jada's father was white, too," Rhonda said. "So
was his mother, I expect. Anyway, Rizzo's been out
of the picture a long while. I don't think he even
knows I'm back in Mansfield."

"Still, I'll need as much information as you can
give me on him." Jordan's headache intensified.
The short list of usual suspects was shrinking fast.
"Any other relatives on your side that we might talk
to?"

"My father was an only child," Rhonda said,
"and he died ten years ago. My younger brother
moved back to Jamaica as soon as he turned 18.
We don't speak much. He's never even met Jada."

That rang alarms in Jordan's ears. International
child trafficking mills would kill—literally—for a
healthy, mixed-race baby. "I'll need all the info you

can share on your brother, too," she said. "Ms. Quarterman, let's check that film. Ms. LeMieux, are you up for this right now?"

Rhonda laid a hand on her friend's arm. "Can— Can Val come with me? For support," she added, gazing at Dawes with tears again streaming down her cheeks.

"I'd be happy to," Dawes said. "If that's okay."

Jordan smiled. "Ms. Dawes," she said, "your first experience as a policewoman may begin much sooner than you expected."

*\*\**

Val sat on Rhonda's right while they viewed the film, one hand on her friend's arm to console her. Val worked hard to suppress her own squeamishness at the intimate touch. But it calmed Rhonda, whose body shook with sobs every time her child's abductor appeared.

Detective Jordan, seated to Rhonda's left, asked Estelle Quarterman to halt the film when the suspect entered, freezing her image in the center of the screen. The film showed the woman's face and body from a top-down angle. The woman seemed to be aware of the camera, as she kept her head bowed, often hiding her face. But the key features she could not hide, such as her brown skin, wavy black hair, and stout figure.

"You don't recognize her?" Jordan asked.

Rhonda shook her head, sobbed more, and squeezed Val's hand.

"She looks nothing like Rhonda," Val said. "She's short, her nose and face are shaped differently, her build—even her skin is much darker."

"My mother was *white*, for the hundredth time," Rhonda said, moaning.

"To be fair, we didn't have a photo of Karina on file," Quarterman said. "And she presented what appeared to be a valid Connecticut driver's license with your mother's name and address."

"Fake IDs are the easiest thing to find around a college campus," Val said. "The counterfeiters practically distribute brochures in the dorms."

"I'll check the usual places," Jordan said. "Estelle, can I get a screenshot of her?"

Quarterman clicked a few keys on her laptop and nodded. "Anything else?"

Jordan sat up in her seat. "A copy of her signature on the sign-out form. Can we check the outside footage?"

Quarterman tapped the keyboard again, and screen displayed the sidewalk in front of the day care center's entrance. A young Latinx couple exited, holding a child, and disappeared into the lot. "This is just before she arrived...and here she is." The suspect stepped into the frame, and the image froze again.

"She's short, all right," Val said. "The other couple was a head taller than her."

"Can we get their contact info?" Jordan said. "They may remember something—her car, anything."

"Here's another angle," Estelle Quarterman said. The screen image shifted to the parking lot. The Latinx couple came into view from behind, and they busied themselves loading their baby into a small SUV. Another vehicle entered, a Toyota sedan with New York plates.

"Freeze it there," Jordan said. "Can anyone

make out the plate number?"

They all squinted at the screen. "They're blurred out," Val said. "I can't read a single number."

"Me either," Rhonda said. "What the hell?"

Jordan sighed. "They mudded the plates. They must've known about the cameras. Dammit! Well, maybe our folks in the lab can make something out. Can I get a copy of this footage?"

Estelle Quarterman smiled and handed the detective a thumb drive. "I expected you to ask for that. There's a scan of the sign-out form and a screenshot of the suspect on there, as well."

"Damn, you're fast," Jordan said. "I'm impressed."

The center director smiled. "When you serve a university community, it pays to keep up with the times."

Jordan stood and stretched, then turned to Rhonda. "I'll run this downtown. Will you come with me? Also, I'll need the names of everyone who knows enough about you and Jada to try something like this—but who wouldn't know what your mother looked like. Can you do that?"

Rhonda shrugged, tears flowing again. "Will I ever see my baby again?" she asked.

Val wrapped an arm around her, steeling herself against the touch, and said in a soft voice, "I'll help you."

Rhonda shook her head. "Thank you, but this isn't your problem. I've involved you too much already."

"Nonsense," Val said. "Call it step one of our research project—partner."

Rhonda's face crumpled again. "You're too kind."

Val hugged her and patted her back, her heart sagging in her chest. She couldn't remember the last time someone called her kind.

It felt good.

# Chapter Four

Val drove Rhonda's Ford Focus to the precinct office, following the detective's rust-colored Charger through slow Mansfield traffic. Rhonda rode with the detective so they could talk further. That afforded Val some alone time, which she used to place a few important calls.

She first called Dominique Hillebrand, head coach of the freshman soccer team. Val dialed the number after stopping at a red light, then set her phone in Rhonda's cup holder and put it on speaker.

"Dawes!" Hillebrand said in greeting. As usual, the coach's voice volume was about ten decibels too loud. "Have you been working on those no-look left-footed passes I showed you? Or is this about taking extra corner kick drills again? I can meet you at three today, if you're available."

"Sorry, Coach," Val said. "Actually, I'm calling to tell you I may have to miss practice today. A friend of mine—"

"Miss practice? No, no, no, no, no," Hillebrand said, her Canadian accent and cadence more pronounced. "Unless you're in the hospital, in class, or in prison…and if you're in class, you know what to do about that."

"I didn't schedule any afternoon classes," Val said. Hillebrand had warned the team to avoid that mistake and had offered to help reschedule around conflicts. Reschedule the class, not practices. "A friend of mine has gotten caught up in a bit of a police situation, and—"

"That's even worse!" Hillebrand huffed and a loud "clunk," similar to a set of weights being dropped on a gym floor, came over the receiver. "You need to steer clear of any police trouble, or any 'friends' who have that sort of issue. The terms of your scholarship are clear on all this. You hear me, Dawes?"

"It's not like that." Val's impatience grew. Her coach's well-earned reputation of shouting first and asking questions later had frustrating consequences. "Someone took her baby from a day care center. I was there when she discovered it, and she needs my help."

"Her baby? Jeez, that's a raw deal." Hillebrand huffed out a noisy breath. "But Dawes, you can't solve everybody else's problems, and you can't go creating them for me and your teammates. Stay clear of anything remotely connected to criminal activity. You understand? Way clear. As in, a hundred percent out."

"It's just for today," Val said, "and probably not even the entire practice. I'll be there if I can, maybe a little late, and I'll be back tomorrow for certain."

"It still counts as an absence," Hillebrand said with a growl. "Another one, and you don't start. Three and you're suspended. Understood?"

Val sighed. "Thanks, coach." She hung up

before any more sarcasm crept into her voice and got her in worse trouble. The coach's harsh response surprised her. Didn't Hillebrand understand that this was a life-or-death situation? Val shook her head, muttering to herself.

Still, she felt partially responsible for Rhonda's predicament. If she hadn't delayed her friend from picking up Jada from day care, none of this would have happened. She wanted to help, but how?

An idea struck her. She voice-commanded her phone to call her brother.

"Chad?" she said when he answered. "Hey, I know you're just starting law school, but could you give me some advice, on behalf of a friend?"

"Hello to you, too, little sister," Chad said, groggy. "And yes, we're all fine here, since you asked. Oh, you *didn't* ask? Silly me." He yawned, a sound that resembled a loud cat's meow.

"Sorry," she said. "How were your first few weeks at Yale?"

"Brilliant," he said. "I haven't slept a wink, and neither has Kendra. Ali's had a stomach bug for the past week, and my first brief is due at 8 a.m. tomorrow. Other than that, law school is pure heaven." He yawned again, not as loud as before.

"I'm sorry," she repeated. "Give that precious girl a hug for me. I'll come visit and help you as soon as I can."

"Don't," he said. "The little diva is contagious right now. Kendra's coming down with it, and I'm fighting it. We'll let you know when it's safe. Now, what's this about your friend?"

Val recounted the events of the morning, fighting tears. "What legal action can she take against her daughter's father once she gets her back?" she asked. "A restraining order, or a ban, or—"

"Whoa, whoa, whoa," Chad said. "First, we don't know if he's responsible. He's the most likely suspect, yes, but as the detective told you, there are other possibilities. Second, a restraining order won't stop someone who's willing to commit a felony—and that's what this sounds like. And third, I'm not a lawyer. I can't offer legal advice to anyone, even you."

"Then take off your lawyer hat," she said, "and just be my big brother. What should I do to help her?"

"Nothing," he said, "other than to be her supportive friend. Console her, keep her calm, hold her hand—figuratively, not literally."

Val's skin grew warm. Chad knew better than most of her aversion to direct human contact.

"But you're not part of this problem, and it could be dangerous if you got involved," he continued. "Guys who do stuff like this tend to turn violent to people who get in their way. Don't become his next victim."

Val rolled her eyes. "Don't pull these 'dangers-of-being-a-cop' scare tactics on me," she said. "I know what I want to do with my life, and your nagging won't dissuade me."

"I'm not trying to change your mind about becoming a cop," he said. "I lost that battle years ago. I'm just saying, you're not a cop, much less a detective. Your jiu jitsu training won't protect you against a guy like that, either."

"I can take care of myself." She failed to keep the defensiveness out of her tone.

"Especially if you make smart choices."

Val seethed. "Would you look at the time? I've got to go. Thanks for, you know. Everything." This time, she did not hide the sarcasm.

"You're welcome," he said, his voice annoyingly cheerful. "By the way, Dad asked about you."

"Interesting that he didn't ask me about me." Distracted, she nearly ran a red light, trying to keep up with the detective. Dammit! She didn't know the location of the precinct office. She'd need to use the GPS in her phone. "Gotta go, bro."

"Love you, sis." This time he sounded sincere.

"Love you too, Chad." She ended the call and opened her phone's maps app, but before she could search for the precinct's address, her phone rang again—an unknown number. "Hello?"

"Miss Dawes. I was wondering if you'd be able to answer from your jail cell."

She recognized the sneering tone of her Criminology professor and sighed. "Dr. Hirsch? What makes you think I'd be in jail?"

"I've had three calls from the local police this morning, asking suspicious questions about your character," he said. "To which I responded, in all honesty, that I can no sooner vouch for you than any Jane, Dick, or hairy Husky on the basketball court. What in heaven's name are you involved in now?"

"I'm not in any trouble," she said. "I'm helping a friend who reported a crime to the police. She's also one of your students, I might add." The light changed, and she set the phone down in the cup holder to drive.

"Oh, *really*?" Hirsch said. "Please, do tell, so I can begin the paperwork to drop the both of you from my class roster. It's awfully difficult to attend college from prison, Miss Dawes."

She sighed, wondering if the man ever made the slightest use of his ears, or whether they were even connected to his brain. "Professor, we're not the ones in trouble. She's the victim, and I'm, well...assisting."

Hirsch snorted. "You'd be of the greatest assistance if you stayed out of the way of the professionals," he said. "Barring that, at least keep them from harassing me with their annoying phone calls. And Dawes? Don't think this encounter with the criminal justice system will help you in my class. It won't. Not one bit."

"Gee, I wouldn't want real-world experience to interfere with my education," she said.

"Good," Hirsch said. The man delivered sarcasm like a pro, but couldn't recognize it in the voices of others. "Because as difficult as it is for women to succeed as police officers, it's impossible for those with a criminal record."

"I don't have a crim—"

"And don't forget," Hirsch said, "your term paper topic selection is due tomorrow afternoon." He hung up without a goodbye.

Val sighed. Perhaps Chad was right about criminology as a field of study. Social work sounded better by the moment.

***

Tanisha Jordan paused in her interview of Rhonda LeMieux to survey her list of potential suspects. Something felt wrong. Rhonda didn't seem upset enough. Most mothers in her position would lose their minds. This one seemed more disconnected than distraught, as if this whole event had happened to someone else. She hadn't spoken ten words in the drive from the day care center to the station and said as little as possible in response to Jordan's questions. It raised her suspicions, to say the least.

She drew in a breath to ask her next question when the door opened and Valorie Dawes entered, escorted by a young officer in uniform. Jordan pointed to an empty chair in the small interview room, an eight-by-twelve rectangle filled by a black-topped table and a handful of uncomfortable chairs. She waited for Dawes to get comfortable, then returned her attention to Rhonda. Perhaps with Dawes in the mix, Rhonda's comfort level would rise and she would open up a little more.

"Besides your brother Desmond, who else in your family might have a connection to Jada?" Jordan asked. "In particular, would any of your relatives resemble the woman on the video?"

Rhonda shook her head and waved Val over to sit next to her. "I don't even have any non-white cousins," she said. "I never met my Jamaican grandparents—they died when my father was still young. As I mentioned, he was an only child."

Jordan took a few notes, mostly to put something on the page. The woman had given her diddly squat to go on. "No other relatives at all?"

Rhonda wagged her head again. "No one that looks anything like her. And my mother's white family wanted nothing to do with us." She made a sour face. "You wouldn't even want me to repeat the names they called her. And me." Tears welled in her eyes again. She squeezed her friend's hand. Dawes seemed uncomfortable with her friend's touch, but remained quiet.

Jordan frowned. Again, no help. "Okay, back to
the baby's father," she said. "What's his last known
place of residence?"

"Rizzo lived in New Haven when we...when I got
pregnant." Her eyes darted over to Dawes, then
toward her lap. "I don't know where he lives now."

"Have you seen Mr. Rizzo since?" Jordan asked.

"No." Rhonda bowed her head.

Dawes cleared her throat. "What about that
night he interrupted you at dinner?" she asked.
"When was that, again?"

Holy crap. Jordan glared at Rhonda. How could
she not remember that? Or thought it important
enough to mention? She wanted to scream at her.
Instead she took a deep, calming breath, and
waited.

"Oh, yeah," Rhonda said, her face brightening a
little. "That was two or three months ago, in
Hartford. I was on a date, and he confronted me.
But he didn't even ask me about the baby."

"Who was this date with?" Jordan tried to mask
her excitement by speaking in a monotone. At last,
something to build on.

"Asher Mulholland. But he wouldn't—"

"I'll need his contact information," the detective
said before Rhonda wasted her time making
excuses for him. Victims often refused to believe
the obvious about the ones they loved. Time to dig
deeper. "How long were you seeing him? Are you
still?"

Dawes winced next to Rhonda, and Jordan
noted that Rhonda had crushed her friend's hands
in a death-like grip. "We went out a few times,"
Rhonda said. "We never got serious."

"Any other boyfriends? Even single dates,

meeting for coffee, a walk in the park. Male or female." Jordan smiled to ease the tension. "I can't assume anything, and neither can you."

Rhonda frowned, a sad expression. "I haven't had a social life since having Jada," she said. "Especially after my mother died. She was my babysitter until she got sick, and I haven't found a replacement. That's why I take her to Little Husky Playpen. But they are so expensive." She bit back tears and seemed to shrink into her seat.

Jordan sighed. Maybe there was nothing there. "Okay. Our hot leads are the brother and Rizzo. We'll check on Mr. Mulholland and follow up with the day care folks, just in case. In the meantime, look at some mugshots. We don't have a lot of middle-aged black females on file, but we might get lucky."

Rhonda's curvy body sagged into her friend's wiry frame. Jordan fixed Dawes with a stare when their eyes met, trying to will her message into the young woman's brain: I need your help here. Dawes seemed to understand, returning Jordan's gaze with a slight nod.

Jordan breathed a bit easier. Dawes had Rhonda's trust, and she struck Jordan as smart, capable, and willing to help. Perhaps she'd inherited some of those same tenacious, intuitive genes that made her uncle such a force in his time.

Maybe, just maybe, Jordan had already gotten a little lucky on this case.

# Chapter Five

Detective Jordan sent Valorie Dawes and Rhonda LeMieux off to review mugshots of middle-aged black female convicts in the area. She didn't expect Rhonda to recognize any of them or match them to the woman in the video, but it was a necessary due diligence step. Meanwhile, Jordan reviewed the security film of the day care center's parking lot with a frustrating result. Whoever had made off with Jada had driven a beige Toyota Camry—one of the most common cars on the road. They'd also mudded over their license plate, rendering it unreadable. The combination made the car almost impossible to find.

"We've got an Amber Alert out on the car, driver, and baby," Jordan said when the three of them gathered in her cramped, dingy office. "Since nobody has made any ransom demands, we have to assume either a family or acquaintance has her, or a trafficking motive. I've alerted the FBI and Interpol, but they won't act until the disappearance hits the 24-hour mark."

"So, what do we do?" Rhonda said, sounding desperate. "Wait until they sell her to the Russians?"

"Like I said, we knock on doors," Jordan said, keeping her voice calm. "And by 'we', I mean the police. As for you, I need you to stand by and be ready to identify anyone we bring in. It will be a little rough on your academic schedule, I'm afraid."

Rhonda burst into tears and collapsed into her chair. "My baby! They have my baby and you sit there, doing nothing!"

Dawes shot Jordan a pleading look and tried to console her friend. The awkward way that she draped her arm around Rhonda told Jordan that Dawes had little to no experience helping others deal with difficult emotions.

"We're doing everything we can," Jordan said in her most patient voice. "But until we find something new, or the abductors make contact, there's not much for either of you to do here."

"So what *should* we do?" Dawes said, her impatience showing. "We can't just sit around and wait for the kidnappers to return the baby with an apology."

"What you need to do next," Jordan said, "is talk to Child Services. There's a rep in a meeting room down the hall—"

"*What?*" Rhonda's voice shrieked off the walls of the tiny room. She stood and leaned over Jordan's desk, glaring down at her. "It's not bad enough that some weirdo walks off with my baby. Now you sic some bureaucrat on me? So, if the kidnappers return her, the state takes her away anyway? No, thank you!"

"I don't think that's what the detective has in mind," Dawes said, though her tone belied her own doubts.

"Right," Jordan said. Good for Dawes, saying the right thing even when she didn't believe it. "Listen, the way these things go is, the kidnappers make you wait, sweat it out a bit. But then they contact you, usually with demands for money and warnings not to go to the police. They want you to get nervous. It makes you more agreeable to their demands."

"And in the meantime?" Dawes and Rhonda said in unison.

"In the meantime," Jordan said with a sigh, "we keep you working so we can stay one step ahead of them. For instance, the Child Services rep will help us find Jada and protect her from harm. They have additional resources to bring to bear. Talk to them. Help them, so they can help us."

Rhonda took a deep breath and looked to her friend for help. Dawes glanced at Jordan, then embraced Rhonda again, this time with a little more grace. "I'll go with you," she said, "to make sure they know you did nothing wrong."

Rhonda wiped the tears from her face, swept her own gaze from Jordan to the detective and back again, and nodded. "Okay," she said. "I'll try. Anything to get Jada back."

"I'll check in on you in a half-hour," Jordan said. "Come on, I'll walk you over there.." She led the two younger women down the hall and knocked on the closed meeting room door, then pushed it open. A squat, forty-something white woman, wearing gold-rimmed glasses and a professional-looking skirt suit, rose out of her chair. Jordan waved Dawes and Rhonda inside.

"Adonna?" she said, and "This is Rhonda LeMieux, the baby's mother, and her friend Valorie Dawes."

"Adonna Matthison, Connecticut Child Services Bureau," the woman said, extending her hand to Rhonda. "Thanks, Tanisha. I'll take it from here."

Jordan eased the door closed, but paused with it open a crack to catch the eye of Dawes as she sat down. "Is this okay?" she mouthed. She tapped her wrist where a watch would be. "You have the time?"

Dawes nodded and gave her a thumbs-up. "We got this," she mouthed back.

Jordan closed the door and strolled back to her office. Dawes, like her uncle, was good people. So far, her talents and helpful intentions had kept Rhonda focused and calm. But including her stretched the bounds of protocol and risked giving Dawes the impression that she should engage further into taking investigative steps. Sooner or later Jordan would have to cut her off, before she became an obstacle to the investigation—and a danger to both of them.

*** 

When the meeting room door closed, Adonna Matthison fixed Val with a concerned frown. "How long have you known Ms. LeMieux?" Matthison asked, taking notes on a tiny laptop.

Val glanced at Rhonda, noted the fear lining her friend's face. "We...met a few weeks ago, in Criminology class."

Matthison frowned and paused in her note-taking and fixed an intense stare on Rhonda. "Are you okay with Miss Dawes being here, Ms. LeMieux? It's a bit unusual, and this could get a bit personal."

Val's heart rate quickened, her blush deepening. Maybe she didn't belong in here. She waited for Rhonda's response.

Doubt joined fear on Rhonda's face. "H-how

personal...what are we going to...why are you here, Ms. Matthison?" Rhonda's voice trembled.

Matthison sighed and gathered her thoughts a moment. "The state has an interest in the child's welfare," she said. "My role is to determine whether we can identify any improvements in her pattern of care that could, ah, keep her safe."

"I'm a good mother!" Rhonda shouted, jumping to her feet. "I love her. I would do anything to keep her safe! You can't take her from me!"

Matthison bit her lip, said nothing.

Val cringed. Nobody could take Rhonda's baby...except a kidnapper. She stood and eased Rhonda back into her chair. "Nobody's saying you're not a good mother," she said, "or that you did something wrong. Right, Ms. Matthison?"

Matthison smiled, an expression so fake Val didn't blame Rhonda for her suspicions. "Nobody's saying anything, yet," the social worker said. "We're here to find out what we can do to keep Jada safe. We all need to stay calm and focus on the facts. Can you do that, Rhonda?"

Val's frustration grew. Matthison's condescension didn't help matters any. She patted Rhonda's arm. "I'll help you, Rhonda. As long as you need me here."

"Actually, that's not your call, nor even Ms. LeMieux's," Matthison said. Her eyes narrowed, and her gaze flitted from Val to Rhonda and back again. "Given what we're about to discuss, I think it best that we continue without Ms. Dawes present."

Fear returned to Rhonda's face. "But I want her here!" she said. "Please?"

Matthison shook her head. "It'd be best if she

weren't present. I'm sorry."

Val cut Rhonda's second protest short. "I'll stay close by," she said. She stood and patted Rhonda's arm. "Call me if you need me." She cast another glance at the social worker, already busy taking notes on her laptop. She gritted her teeth and sucked in a deep breath. Damned passive-aggressive control freaks.

But on the off-chance that it could help find Jada sooner, Val needed to go along. She shuffled out and closed the door behind her. Some twenty feet down the hall, she found an empty meeting room and pulled her laptop and Research Methods text out of her backpack. Might as well use the time to catch up on homework.

Some fifteen minutes later, Rhonda flew past the room, sobbing. By the time Val reached the doorway, Rhonda had disappeared from sight.

\*\*\*

Val approached the open door of the small conference room that Rhonda had exited moments before and knocked. Adonna Matthison started, as if she'd been absorbed in deep thought.

"Ah, Ms. Dawes. Come in." She shook her head and tsk'd. "I hoped to see Ms. LeMieux, but perhaps you and I should chat now."

Val drew a deep breath and retook her seat. "I take it your talk didn't go well," she said.

"These situations are always fraught with emotion," Matthison said. "Ms. LeMieux's reaction is not at all unusual."

Unease bubbled near the surface in Val's chest. This woman showed no empathy for Rhonda's understandable fears and frustration. Her friend needed help, not psychoanalysis. Val licked her lips, searching for the right words. "What happened?"

Matthison smiled and removed her glasses, a half-smile softening her stark features. "Ms. LeMieux got a little defensive. But I am not here to accuse anyone," she said. "My sole objective is to do what's best for the child. Sometimes, that requires I ask some tough questions. It can be difficult for a parent to hear."

"Still," Val said, her throat tight, "put yourself in her place. Jada is missing. Any number of individuals might have taken her, including some terrible people. She's afraid and angry. Wouldn't you be?"

"Of course," Matthison said. "She should receive counseling to help her through this. But that's not my role. Nor is it to locate the child. Mine is to ensure that when Jada is returned to her—if she is returned—"

"It's those types of statements that add to Rhonda's distress," Val said. "Maybe she doesn't need to hear things like that."

Matthison's smile faded. "We don't have time to tiptoe around this situation," she said. "It's serious, and dangerous. Rhonda's anger at me will subside, but only if this is all resolved successfully—which means, quickly. Can you help us with that?"

"Of course," Val said. "That's why I'm here. How can I help?"

Matthison clicked on her keyboard a moment. "Can you help clarify something for me? You went with Ms. LeMieux to the day care center this morning, correct? What time did you arrive?"

Val searched her memory. "Around 10:20," she said. "I recall Rhonda worrying that we were late."

Matthison removed her glasses to clean them and glanced at Val. "Could it have been later? Say, 10:23?"

Val held her breath a moment. "Maybe," she said. "What difference do those three minutes make? The kidnappers took Jada at 9:50, a full half-hour before."

"Did Ms. LeMieux share with you what time she was due at the center to pick up Jada?" Matthison said in a condescending tone.

Val's stomach churned. Matthison's question was intended as a trap! "She didn't," Val said, "but if I do the math, I'd guess it was 10:15?"

"Correct. Thank you for confirming that she was late...again." She put her glasses back on and typed on her keyboard.

Val watched her work, dumbstruck at her bureaucratic demeanor. "So, that's it?" she said. "All that matters is closing the case? Not how it affects people?"

"How it affects the child is my top concern," Matthison said, her eyes glued to her screen. "All else is secondary."

"Really?" Val shook her head in wonder. So clinical. "The only measure of success is whether you're satisfied with who gets custody of the baby?"

"Not just who, but the overall care that person can provide," Matthison said, still typing.

"Isn't the child's mother the best person to provide that care?" Val asked.

"Most often, but not always." Tap, tap, tap.

"That all sounds so...I don't know, impersonal,"

Val said. "What about the child's happiness? Or Rhonda's?"

Matthison pushed her laptop aside and squared off to face Val. "How would I measure happiness, Miss Dawes?" She smiled and folded her hands on the table. "In my line of work, success and failure are difficult, sometimes impossible, to measure. Often we don't know if we've made the right decision for a child for decades—maybe never. Does he or she grow up to be a well-functioning, successful adult? And how would I measure that? Would a different choice have yielded a more satisfactory result? We can't say for sure. All we have are studies and case histories of what people have tried in the past, and their results. Even those data are incomplete and imperfect. No two children, and no two families, are alike. It's conjecture, Miss Dawes. Unfortunate, but true."

Val took a moment to digest Matthison's speech. The words all seemed logical and well-supported, but it depressed her. "So, that's the life of a social worker?" she said. "Uncertain guesswork, with no way of knowing if you've made the right choice?"

Matthison's lips curled upward into a sad smile. "It's not all negative," she said. "We do affect lives, I hope in a positive way. We don't always get to see it personally. Clients don't return to our offices to tell us they've stayed out of jail or kicked their drug habits, for example. But we learn to observe successes in other ways. Names stop appearing in the system. A family gets by without public assistance. A foster child finds a permanent home. These are our 'wins', Miss Dawes. They don't happen often enough, but when they do, we celebrate them."

Val sank back into her chair, a lump rising in her throat. She'd considered social work as an alternative career path, thinking it would give her the chance to better the lives of those who most needed support. In her idealized vision, she'd delight in watching her clients escape their difficult situations and prosper. She'd envisioned that as a more positive approach versus policing, which focused on punishing those who did wrong.

But Adonna Matthison painted a picture of social work that appeared just as bleak, with even fewer opportunities to witness the beneficial impact of her efforts.

Now, neither career path offered her hope of achieving the personal and professional satisfaction she sought.

With that realization, a heavy weight settled over her, and the world became a much darker place.

# Chapter Six

Val found Rhonda outside, pacing in the parking lot. "No cops and no government are gonna take away my baby," she shouted over and over. No matter how soothing Val's tone and words, Rhonda refused to believe that anyone inside the station—especially Adonna Matthison—had her best interests at heart. Nor Jada's.

After her meeting with Matthison, Val couldn't blame her.

"Your government's no better than Jamaica's," Rhonda said once she stopped yelling. "They do what's good for them, and nobody else."

"What do you want to do, then?" Val said. "How will you find her if you don't trust the police to help?"

"I'll go find Rizzo myself," Rhonda said. "It can't be that hard. He isn't smart enough to hide from me."

"But what if it wasn't Rizzo that took her?" Val said. "You said yourself, he doesn't even know you're in Mansfield."

"If he doesn't have her, he'll help me find her," Rhonda said. "And God save the bastards when Rizzo finds them. He gets mean when he's mad."

"Let the police and the state help you," Val said. "They've done this before, and—"

"You know what else they've done before?" Rhonda said, shouting again. "Take poor babies from their mothers. Put black people in jail for 'losing' their kids. You think the Man is looking out for you? Maybe so, for a white girl. Not for a girl like me!" She jumped in her car and started the engine. Before Val could react, Rhonda's Ford Focus zoomed out of the parking lot and into traffic.

Val stared after her for a long moment, then sighed and trudged inside. She knocked on Tanisha Jordan's office door moments later.

"Things didn't go well with Child Services, I hear," Jordan said. "Where's Rhonda?"

"Gone," Val said. "Apparently, she thinks she can find Jada better on her own."

"Oh, hell," Jordan said, picking up her desk phone. "That's such a bad idea. Where's she headed?"

"To find Rizzo," Val said. "I'm guessing New Haven."

Jordan cursed and punched a few buttons into her phone's keypad. After a moment, she said into the receiver, "Stork's left the nest. Yeah, the missing baby case. Did you get her vehicle data, plates, all that? Good. Yeah, put the word out. No, don't bring her in. Just monitor her and keep me posted. Thanks." She slammed the phone into its cradle. "That makes things harder. Hey, why didn't she bring you with her?"

"I guess she doesn't trust me, either," Val said.

Jordan shot her a rueful smile. "Get used to it," she said. "If you're serious about becoming a cop someday, that is."

"I had a whole different experience with law

enforcement growing up, thanks to my uncle," she said. "When I think of the police, I picture him. Kind, strong, principled, helpful. No cop ever gave me reason to mistrust them."

"Yeah, well," Jordan said, "your experience is a lot different than most people of color. I get Rhonda's paranoia, to some extent. Growing up, I felt it too."

"But you got over it, right?" Val said. "I mean, look at you now."

Jordan snorted. "Yeah, I got over that paranoia, only to replace it with a different kind." She shook her head. "Think long and hard about this profession, Ms. Dawes. It's often not friendly to women."

"In what way?" Val sunk into Jordan's guest chair. "If you don't mind sharing."

Jordan narrowed her eyes and pointed to her office door. Val closed it and waited.

"Police work is a man's game," Jordan said. "At least, that's how the men feel, and in some ways, they're right. It's grueling, physical, and tough. Have you ever been in a fight?"

Val shrugged. "Not per se. But I trained in jiu jitsu, black belt. So I've taken a few punches."

"But not from someone who meant you actual harm." Jordan's computer beeped, and she turned back to read the screen.

"Well..." Val's voice quivered and dropped to a whisper. "I have been...*assaulted* before."

*The large man stood over her, his heavy breathing filling the room over the distorted sounds of the TV blaring downstairs. He reached out and grabbed the covers of her bed. She tried to scream, but no sound would come—and nobody was home to hear her. The man's face contorted into a cruel, sickening smile as he ripped the blankets off of her—*

Val shuddered at the memory. She had no intention of sharing that story with the detective— or anyone.

Jordan, however, seemed not to have heard Val's response or noticed her shutdown reaction. "Sooner or later," she said, "you'll get into it with a guy twice your size whose momma never taught him not to hit girls. Trust me, punches hurt, Dawes. They hurt a lot."

Val shuddered again. It hurt to get *assaulted*, too, in that unique way that men assault women to assert their power, the dominance of their gender—

"But that's not the worst part," Jordan continued. "To me, the worst is how the male cops treat you. Not all, but enough of them."

Val cleared her throat and shook off the awful memory. "That's mostly the senior guys, though, right?" Val said. "The old guard?"

"Hah!" Jordan said. "I suppose, in general, the old coots are more traditional in that regard. But I'm shocked every day by what even the younger guys get away with."

"They harass you?" Val asked, surprised. Despite her surprise, she was glad to focus on anything other than her childhood trauma.

Jordan scoffed. "If only they were that overt. Sure, sometimes they'll pinch your butt or crack a crude joke, but those are the exceptions. Usually it's more subtle than that. They don't trust that you're big or tough enough, that you can do the job as well as they can. You won't be 'one of the guys,' ever. They'll pass you over for opportunities, for promotions. After a while, you wonder if it's all worth it."

Val sat up straighter in her chair. "Well?" she said. "Is it?"

Jordan smiled at her. "For me, it has been," she said. "But I'll tell you the truth. I came into it with a chip on my shoulder, wanting to prove I was every bit as good as they were. I worked twice as hard and took twice as much crap as they ever would. Maybe four times as much, to make up for me not being white and male. But I also had...let's just say, I was extra motivated to get out of my situation, compared to most people."

Val exhaled, for the first time realizing she'd been holding her breath during Jordan's speech. "If you had to do it over again," she said, "would you?"

Jordan stared at her for several seconds. "I don't know, Dawes," she said. "I'm glad I did, because I've learned a lot. We need women in the police ranks to educate these fools. But would I want to repeat all that I've been through?" She shook her head. "Not on your life."

Val left Jordan's office in a deep funk, and not only about the sadness she felt for Rhonda and the strain in their nascent friendship. Adonna Matthison had soured her impression of social work, and now Tanisha Jordan had done the same for law enforcement. Val's career options seemed cloudier than ever—and so far, she'd done nothing to help Rhonda get her daughter back.

***

Minutes after Valorie Dawes left the detective's office, a knock interrupted Jordan's quiet concentration at her keyboard. A tall, white-haired uniformed male cop pushed the door open a moment later. "Detective," he said, "A Mr. Mulholland is here to speak with you."

"Show him in." Jordan's pulse quickened. Finally, someone might offer significant information about LeMieux's past other than Rhonda herself. Asher Mulholland could help fill in key details and verify others. And while his showing up at a police station voluntarily reduced the odds of his being the perpetrator, she couldn't rule it out just yet.

Rhonda had described him as tall and athletic, but that didn't prepare Jordan for the fine specimen of manhood that strolled into her office moments later. Jordan estimated Mulholland at six-five, 220 or 230, with a muscular build and a confident grace in his movements. "Have a seat," she said after introducing herself and shaking his hand. He held on with a firm but not crushing grip and graced her with a shy, boyish smile.

"I expected Rhonda would be here," he said. "Is there any word about Jada?"

"We're making progress," Jordan said, her standard phrase no matter what state her case was in. "Mr. Mulholland, where were you between nine and eleven o'clock this morning?"

"At my office in Hartford—Constitution Finance and Equity—meeting with clients," Mulholland said. "The firm's receptionist can provide confirmation. But you don't think I'm responsible, do you?"

Jordan shrugged. "You've seen a bit of trouble in your time, Mr. Mulholland. Care to explain?"

He took the seat she'd offered and expelled a loud breath of air. "I was a fighter as a kid," he said. "Competitive boxer, but also, outside of the ring. Dudes in the 'hood often challenged guys like me, see if we're as tough on the street as in the gym." He shook his head. "Once I got carried away and hurt a guy. I did my time and cleaned myself up. My record should show that." His eyes glowed with a fiery intensity.

She looked away before he did, a little ashamed of her assumptions. Keep an open mind, she reminded herself. "We can't rule anything out yet," she said. "What is your current relationship with Rhonda LeMieux?"

"We have no current relationship to describe." Sadness etched the corners of his voice. "We dated a few times, but I guess the chemistry never happened...at least for her. I like Rhonda very much."

Jordan nodded. Besides his handsome face and impressive build, his soft-spoken manner and soothing baritone put her right at ease. She had difficulty understanding why Rhonda wouldn't have kept dating him. "And Jada?"

He stared at her with a blank expression, then recognition dawned. "Her daughter? Sad to say, I've never met her," he said. "Our relationship never progressed to where Rhonda felt it appropriate."

Jordan nodded. So far, it all lined up with Rhonda's version of the story. "What can you tell me about Marty Rizzo?"

Mulholland's eyes darkened. "Rizzo crashed our

first date and demanded visitation rights to their child. He was rude and obnoxious, and I don't see what Rhonda saw in him."

Jordan laughed. "I meet a lot of those guys in my line of work," she said.

He smiled and seemed to relax. Good. "I bet you do," he said. "Not so much in mine."

"And what do you do for Constitution Finance?" Jordan blushed, hoping her question didn't come across as too personal. Dammit, she had a boyfriend, a nice guy who put up with all the crap that a policewoman brought home. She resolved to put up a stronger fight to resist Mulholland's looks and charm.

"I help people manage individual investment accounts," he said. "I met Rhonda as a client, when she inherited a little money after her mother died."

"So you know her net worth," Jordan said, in a tone that came off more accusatory than she intended.

He surrendered a wry smile. "Her bank balance wouldn't justify risking life in prison over. Mr. Rizzo, however, seems to have a different impression."

"How so?" Jordan took a few notes. This was getting interesting.

Mulholland frowned. "When he showed up at our dinner date, he accused Rhonda of stealing Jada's inheritance, which he claimed was his, as the baby's father," he said. "Never mind how ridiculous *that* sounds. The sum of money we're talking wouldn't buy a house in the suburbs, much less the wealth he imagined. I don't know where he came up with this crazy idea that her mother left her millions. The woman taught fourth grade, for heaven's sake. What little remained after her battle with cancer went into a trust for Jada and a small stipend for Rhonda and her brother. And when I say small, I mean a few thousand dollars."

"Was that your only interaction with Mr. Rizzo?" Jordan asked, feeling like the interview might wrap up too soon. But eye candy or not, she couldn't afford to waste time—hers, or Asher's.

"No," Mulholland said, his voice dropping in pitch. "I never told Rhonda this, but Rizzo stalked me for a while. One night, he jumped me and threatened to kick the hell out of me if I didn't stay away from her."

"Did you?"

He grimaced. "It was all moot. Rhonda had already broken things off by then. He called me a liar, started pushing me around a little."

"How did that work out for him?" Jordan asked, grinning. "Let me guess. Unlike you, Rizzo never boxed competitively."

He laughed. "Mr. Rizzo has a glass jaw. But I won't be sharing the details of how I found that out, Detective."

She grew serious again. "You wouldn't have current contact information for Mr. Rizzo, do you?" she asked.

Mulholland reached into his pocket and pulled out a cell phone. "Number one on my Blocked Caller list. I'd only be too happy to share his contact information with you."

Writing down the details, Detective Jordan celebrated inside. Finally, something broke her way.

# Chapter Seven

Val made it to the last hour of soccer practice and ran twice as hard as usual—even for her—to make up for what she'd missed. Coach Hillebrand waved off Val's explanation but assigned her to scrimmage with the second team. Afterwards, the coach ordered Val to take an extra dozen laps after practice, which she did without complaint. After Val showered, the coach smacked her butt with a towel and jerked a thumb over her shoulder.

"Hurry, Dawes," she said. Hyperactive as always, Hillebrand's 5'8" athletic frame appeared to bounce in place while she stood. "I've got dinner plans. And some woman by the name of Rhonda is outside."

"Did she say anything about her daughter being found?" Val asked, heart racing. She kept her breathing even, not wanting to inhale too much of the locker room's sweaty, fungal aromas.

Hillebrand scowled and ran her fingers through her spiky, blue-and-white hair. "I'm not your social secretary, Dawes," she said with a growl. "Is this the one who made you late today?"

Val nodded. "Sorry, coach, I—"

"Save it." Hillebrand fluttered her hands toward the lockers. "Come on, get going. I don't have all night."

Val sucked in a deep breath, bit back a snarky retort, and hurried to her locker. She dressed in a rush, eschewing make-up, as always, and had almost reached the exit when Hillebrand called to her again.

"Dawes!" The coach stood outside the door to her cramped office, bordered on two sides by oversized glass panes. "This friend with the missing baby. Is her name Lee-moo?"

"LeMieux," Val said, nodding. "Why?"

Hillebrand pointed to a TV affixed to the top of the wall opposite her desk. "You've made the news."

"Crap!" Val scurried into the office to listen to the broadcast. The screen showed Detective Jordan speaking with a reporter alongside a grainy photo of the woman who'd taken Jada. Jordan said something about asking for anyone who recognized her to call the toll-free number on the bottom of the screen.

"Don't get dragged into this mess, Dawes," Hillebrand said. "I mean it."

"You don't think I should help my friend find her missing baby?" Val said. "Seriously?"

"Let the police handle it," Hillebrand said. "Remember what I said about your scholarship. We don't need scandals like this attached to UConn soccer."

Val's mouth dropped open and her ears flushed red. "There won't be any scandal," she said. "But I won't let money stand in the way of saving a child's life!" She pushed past the coach and fled out of the locker room.

She calmed down about halfway to the building's exit. Great move, dummy, she scolded herself. Alienating the woman who controlled her financial lifeline at college—for what? She'd done nothing of substance so far to help Rhonda.

Still. She would never bail on a friend in need.

Val found Rhonda leaning against her car in a parking lot outside the practice facility. "I'm so sorry for how I acted earlier today," Rhonda said, her face a well of sadness. "I was just so upset about Jada, and that Child Services lady seemed to blame me for it, and—"

"No need to apologize," Val said. "Is there any word?"

"Rizzo's gone missing," Rhonda said. "He lost his job, and his landlord hasn't seen him in over a week. I'm certain he's involved in this, Val. But I don't know—oh, damn, there's my cell." A tinny, muted version of Bob Marley's "Don't Worry About a Thing" played from Rhonda's purse. She yanked her phone out and answered it. "Desmond!" she said. "I've been trying to reach you!"

A man's voice shouted into Rhonda's ear, the strong Jamaican accent distorting the words enough to make them unintelligible for Val. Rhonda shook her head. "But Desm—" More shouting. Rhonda sent Val a pleading look.

"I can't tell what he's saying," Val said in a low voice.

Rhonda frowned and put the call on speaker. Desmond's Jamaican lilt filled the air. "Then they said they'd kill me!" he shouted. "And I didn't do nothing!"

"Who said they'd kill you?" Val said. "When?"

"Who's that with you?" Desmond's voice shrilled with suspicion and fear. "Rhonda, I just told you, we can't tell anybody anything!"

"My friend, who's helping me," Rhonda said. "Who were these men? What did you tell them?"

"They were looking for you." Desmond's voice grew more agitated. "Yesterday morning. I didn't tell them anything, I swear!"

Val stared at Rhonda. "That means they're the ones who—Desmond. What did they want with Rhonda?"

"Where she's living, who she's dating, stuff like that," he said. "They just said if I didn't tell them, they'd cut off my fingers, then my toes, then my...I can't even say it. They'll kill me, Rhonda! What should I do?"

"Cooperate with the police, that's what," Rhonda said. "They're also looking for you."

"No! No cops!" Desmond's voice reached pure panic mode. "They said if I contact the cops—"

"The police will protect you," Val said. "These men can't reach you there."

"Ha!" Desmond said. "Maybe in Connecticut, but in Jamaica—"

"Hush!" Rhonda said. "Desmond! Do not say where I am out loud, to anyone, ever! You didn't tell these men where I am, even by accident, did you?"

"No! I swear!" The line grew silent for a moment. "I don't think."

"You don't *think*?" Rhonda held the phone out wide from her body and stared at the ground, seething. "Desmond!" she shouted. "What–did–you–say–*exactly*?"

"Nothing!" he said, wailing. "I didn't tell them

nothing!"

Rhonda seethed again, shaking her head at the ground, speechless.

"What questions did they *ask* you?" Val said.

"Where Rhonda was, and where the baby goes for day care, things like that," Desmond said. "I said I didn't know, but they didn't believe me. They took out a knife and held my hand down and— and—Rhonda, they were going to cut off my thumb," he said, sobbing.

"So...you told them?" Rhonda's voice had regained an eerie calm. "You told them where I was?"

"I said you were living in Mother's house," Desmond said. "But they knew that wasn't true. Then I told them you went back to Yale. They said if they find out that's a lie, they will be back. Rhonda, what am I gonna do?"

"Go to the cops, like my friend here said you should," Rhonda said. "Otherwise, keep your mouth shut!" She hung up the phone and pressed her hands to her head. "That's how they found me, then. Rizzo knew I couldn't go back to Yale, but it probably wasn't hard to figure out I'd switched to UConn. Closer to my mother's house, and all that. That stupid boy!"

Val nodded in agreement, but gestured for Rhonda to sit on the car's hood next to her. "You can't blame Desmond for trying to save his own skin," she said. "At least we have a lead, now. The police can get a description of the men in Jamaica and trace them back to here. It doesn't sound it, but this is a good development, to my way of thinking."

Rhonda glared at her. "That's because," she said

between her teeth, "you're not missing an eighteen-month-old baby." She jumped into her Ford Focus and started the engine. Val had just enough time to tumble off the hood before the car lurched backward out of the parking space and sped out of the lot.

Panting on her hands and knees on the pavement, Val stared after her, disappearing at high speed down the narrow road leading off campus. Her friend's volatile reactions put both of them in greater danger, so long as Val continued to help. Coach Hillebrand's warning echoed in her head: *Don't get involved.* Part of her saw the wisdom in her coach's words.

But only a small part. The rest focused on the picture in her mind of eighteen-month-old Jada, and the danger she was in. If something similar happened to her niece, Ali, she'd want someone—everyone—to do everything they could to help. She couldn't abandon her friend. Rhonda's impulsiveness made her even more vulnerable—and more than ever, in need of a friend like Val.

# Chapter Eight

The sun drifted below the tops of the trees bordering the parking lot, casting long shadows on the pavement, but bringing a welcome, partial relief from the day's intense heat. Val slung her backpack over her shoulder and trudged toward her dorm, clear across campus. To save time, she cut through the natatorium that bordered the practice facility. Holding her breath against the heavy aroma of chlorine and sweat, she focused on ways she could help Rhonda in this impossible situation. She exited the building and waited for some cars to pass before crossing Hillside Avenue.

About a hundred yards south, a swarthy man in a dark jacket and slacks ducked behind the pillars supporting the east entrance of the basketball pavilion.

The man raised her suspicions for a few reasons. One, the furtive movement, as if he were hiding. Two, the dark jacket, far too heavy for the unseasonably warm September evening.

She glanced in his direction again, but didn't spot him. Either he'd hidden well, or she'd imagined it, or he'd continued on inside the building. Maybe it wasn't a jacket, after all. It might have been a basketball player wearing a navy blue UConn sweatshirt, heading in to practice.

Except that athletes didn't use the main entrance, and the team didn't practice in the pavilion.

Val jogged across the street, glancing back at the pavilion entrance. Her legs still ached from three hours of running, but adrenaline quieted the pain. She made it past the engineering building without further visual evidence of the man, and she slowed to a walk again. She rounded the corner and glanced up at the windows of the art museum—

She saw him again. A stocky man in his mid-twenties, about 5'7" tall, with dark, curly hair. The shadows hid key facial details, even his skin color, especially with the sun in her eyes. But he more or less matched Rhonda's description of Rizzo. He seemed to be trying to blend in, without success, among the students ambling down the sidewalk along the open green.

Val broke into a run—no jogging this time—brushing past a few clusters of students walking abreast on the sidewalk. The road curved right, and a giant, stately oak screened her enough to risk stealing another glance back at the man, but she'd lost sight of him. It looked familiar: she'd cut through this courtyard early that morning on her way to calculus class. She knew her way around, now. She detoured through the science complex, hoping to lose him among the maze of buildings crowding the north end of the campus. Looked back again—

And lost her footing in one of the giant, unrepaired holes in the concrete walk, falling flat on her face on the sidewalk. Her backpack opened, and her sociology book, pens, and notepad scattered everywhere. Luckily, her Chromebook didn't fall out and get destroyed on the concrete. A few students snickered, and someone let out a "Whoa!" No one helped her up, or to gather her things. She rushed through that, keeping her eye to the south, where she'd last seen him.

He ducked behind a white van parked on the side of the road. Trying to hide, but staying close.

Val considered her options. The police—and Rhonda—were looking for Rizzo, to question him, if not arrest him. She needed to notify them, fast, without alerting him. Tough to do, with him watching her—unless she could get inside her dorm, still a few blocks away, before he caught up to her. Under normal circumstances, her track-star speed would make that a simple task, but soccer practice had turned her legs to rubber. And he'd closed the distance behind her to less than 50 yards.

A new thought struck her: if Rizzo had taken Jada, where was the child now? With the woman who'd picked her up from day care, she assumed. That meant Rizzo trusted her, as he would only leave his prized possession with a close partner. That narrowed the possibilities. The police should be able to track down the woman's identity quickly and, with that, Jada's location.

Unless they'd already moved her out of the area. Or hurt her—

Val pushed that option out of her mind. Think positive: the kidnappers needed Jada safe and healthy. Particularly Rizzo, the child's father.

She decided on a new strategy: keep her

pursuer close enough to know his location at all
times, but distant enough that he couldn't hurt or
threaten her. A tricky balance, given her tired legs,
but she'd manage, somehow.

The second part of her strategy: get help,
without scaring him away.

Val pulled out her cell and Tanisha Jordan's
business card. She had little to lose by calling
Rizzo in. So what if he saw her making a call?
Worst case, she could still outrun him. Probably.

"You've reached Detective Tanisha Jordan,
Mansfield Police Department," the voice at the
other end of the line greeted her. Voice mail! "You
know what to do." A beep followed.

"Detective, this is Val Dawes. Rizzo's following
me. I'm almost to my dorm. I'll call again—"

Hard-pounding footsteps sounded behind her.
Another glance confirmed her fear: the man was
running toward her. She shoved the phone into her
pocket and raced ahead, but the backpack and her
tired legs slowed her.

Val hurried down a covered walkway that
snaked along the biology building, then ran up the
broad steps at the far end. At the top, breathing
hard, she looked for him again. No luck, but he
might have hidden among the large, pale-yellow
concrete columns bordering each side. She raced
down the busy street that sliced through campus,
separating the dorms from the academic clusters.
A break in traffic allowed her to cross. On the other
side lay a cemetery, surrounded by a low stone
wall, not quite waist high on her. She could cut
through, but it meant leaving the comfort of
people—potential witnesses—behind.

Another check-in with her pursuer revealed that

he'd gained some ground. He must have run up the stairs, too. But he hadn't made it across the street yet. The man looked right at her, no longer hiding his intent to follow. Val needed to push herself harder if she planned to maintain a safe distance. But her leg muscles burned, and try as she might, she could not move any faster.

Which meant, shortening the distance.

She dashed toward the wall, pacing herself as if she were running the 440 hurdles. Timing her leap, she pushed off the ground, extending her legs wide.

But she'd misjudged the depth of the stone wall, and her trailing leg scraped the wall's sharp edge. She lost her balance and face-planted in the turf, rolling to a stop against one of the gnarly trees that lined the grounds. Her head tapped the trunk's base, and for a moment, she saw stars.

Then, she saw the dark-haired man dodging traffic, racing toward her.

Val sprang to her feet and dashed among the headstones toward the Episcopalian chapel, about 100 yards east. She reached top sprinting speed in seconds and did not look back. She timed her jump over the stone wall perfectly this time and raced across the lawn to the paved path that led up the hill to her dormitory. Students crowded the walk, chatting and laughing, forcing her to slow her pace. With heavy breaths, she strode up the hill, nearing the steps that would bring her to the residential courtyard.

"Hey!" someone exclaimed behind her. "Quit pushing. What's your problem, mister?"

Sure enough, the man had continued his bold pursuit, now with no pretense of hiding.

A blue emergency phone tower rose from the ground at the intersection of the sidewalk and steps. She recalled from freshman orientation that pressing the tower's large red button would initiate a 9-1-1 call—if it worked. At any given time, some ten to fifteen percent of the units were out of order. Most of the broken units were hooded, once the breakdown was detected. This one wasn't.

She pushed her way to it and pressed the button. Waited a heartbeat or two. Nothing. She pressed it again, harder, and glanced left, back toward the stocky man in pursuit. Took another breath—

A blue light on the top of the pole began blinking.

Val didn't wait for the phone to dial campus police. Instead, she dashed up the first flight of stairs. Where the stairway turned to the right, she glanced back. The man chasing her had paused in his pursuit, staring wide-eyed at the blinking beacon.

Val continued up the steps, past the first dormitory with its circular corner tower of multi-colored glass panels, and headed to her own dorm building. She eased her pace to a brisk walk and, glancing around, breathed a sigh of relief: she'd lost him.

She pulled out her phone again and punched in the numbers: 9—1—

The phone rang. Detective Jordan's number appeared on the screen.

"Detective!" She said. "Rizzo's here! Less than sixty yards away from me! What do you want me to do?"

"Are you home yet?" Jordan asked.

"Almost," Val said. "Just a few hundred—"

"Get inside," Jordan said. "Fast."

"Shouldn't I stay in sight so that Rizzo—"

"That's not Rizzo," Jordan said. "Get inside!"

"Wait, what?" Val hurried to the dorm's rear entrance. Fast footsteps echoed off the pavement behind her. "Are you sure? He meets the description—"

"I know it for a fact," Jordan said. "Now get! In! *Side!*"

"How can you be certain?" Val said, sliding her ID into the security card reader and yanking open the door.

"Because," Jordan said, "Marty Rizzo is about fifty feet from me right now. Sitting in a jail cell."

The door closed behind Valorie, and she whirled to peek through the window to find the man who'd been chasing her. But the green yard in front of the dorm remained empty. Whoever the man was, he'd given up the chase.

# Chapter Nine

Tanisha Jordan pushed open the door of the tiny interrogation room and made a point of ignoring the stocky, olive-skinned man handcuffed to the metal chair behind a table. Marty Rizzo's black, curly hair stuck to his scalp and a sheen of sweat lined his clean-shaven face. The temperature in the room probably exceeded 90, maybe 100. Sweltering. Good.

She slung her jacket over the back of her own chair and set a folder stuffed with printouts on the table. She nodded once at the mirrored-glass wall behind her. A slight flickering of the lights signaled that yes, the observation team was ready. She poured water from a plastic pitcher into a paper cup. "Thirsty?"

Rizzo sneered at her. "You know I can't reach it." He shook his hands to rattle the cuffs behind him.

"Be a good boy and maybe I can fix that." She poured another cup and took a sip, then sat down. "So, Marty, what brings you to Mansfield?" She kept her tone light, conversational. Lower the tension a bit.

No luck. "Call me Rizzo," he said. "Everybody does."

"Your friends, you mean?" She chuckled. "Does that make me your friend, Marty?"

Rizzo scowled at her. "Who are you? You a cop?"

She laughed. "Who else skips dinner and hangs out at police stations at night? Oh, yeah." She leaned across the table and gritted her teeth. "Convicts, like you."

"Is that why you brought me here?" he asked, nonchalant. "To read me my rap sheet? Thanks, but I don't need reminders. And I ain't done anything, so—"

"Where's Jada?" Not accusatory, just matter-of-fact. *Give up the facts and we all go home.* "Who's watching her right now?"

"I don't know," he said. "I didn't take her."

"Ah, but you're aware that she's missing," Jordan said. "So who did it? Friend of yours? Hired hand?"

"I saw it on the news," he said. "So I came to talk to Rhonda, and to help find my daughter. Wouldn't you?"

"Where were you this morning, between, say, nine and eleven a.m.?" Jordan opened her folder and wrote the date and time on a blank interview form. "Specifically."

"Working."

"Where? For whom?"

"A construction site in Hartford. My boss can vouch for me."

"Boss's name?" She took notes on the form.

"Joe."

She grunted in exasperation. "Is there only one Joe in Hartford?"

"Rizzo." He grinned. "My uncle."

"How convenient that your Uncle Joey can

vouch for you."

"The other guys on the crew can, too," Rizzo said. "I worked until four and heard the news about Jada on the drive home. I showered and came straight to Mansfield. Honest to God."

Jordan rolled her eyes. "When is the last time you've been honest to God, or anyone else, about anything?" She tapped her pen on the almost-blank page. "Give me Uncle Joey's number."

He did. "Joe can give you the names and numbers of the other guys."

"Who's this?" Jordan slid a photo across the table of the woman who'd picked up Jada from day care, a grainy shot lifted from the video.

Rizzo shook his head. "No idea."

"Never seen her before, ever?"

"Nope. I don't hang with n—I mean, uh, no."

Heat rose in Jordan's face. "What were you about to say, Marty?" She waited, but got no reply. "You don't hang with *black people*, is that it?"

"What about it?" he said. "So I don't know many of you people. Women, anyway. The guys I work with are all right."

She controlled her anger enough to keep her voice level. "You made at least one exception."

Rizzo stared at her with a blank expression, then recognition dawned. "Oh, you mean Rhonda. Well, not really. I mean, she's only half. And we had one good night, you hear what I'm saying?" He grinned, and stale, rank air escaped from his mouth. Jordan edged away from him and held her breath for a few moments. "But," Rizzo continued, "she won't have nothing to do with me now. Won't even let me see my daughter."

"The courts appear to agree with her." Jordan

pulled a restraining order from the file. "You're in violation even being in the city."

He shrugged. "Somebody took my daughter. It was worth the risk."

She sighed. He was either lying, dumb, or both. "You have a history of stalking her."

"I didn't stalk her," he said, his voice rising. "I saw her out on a date—in Hartford, where I live. It was an accident."

"You approached her, interrupted her dinner, confronted her—"

"I got mad, okay? It bugged me to see her with him." His tone softened. "I didn't like the idea of some other guy replacing me as father to my child. But I said my piece and left."

"You mean you noticed how big her date was and ran away?" Jordan couldn't suppress a smile at Rizzo's expense. "Typical bully. So tough, until a bigger dude comes along."

"That's not how it happened!"

"Who am I going to believe?" Jordan raised her voice. "A convict? Or a college-educated, professional man with a clean slate?" She bit her lip at the fib about Asher's record. A little white lie that didn't matter.

"I don't care what you believe," Rizzo said. "About then, or now. Bust me for the R.O. violation if you want, but you've got nothing else. And I swear, I want the same thing you and Rhonda do. Jada, safe and back home."

"Then why'd you take her?"

"I DIDN'T TAKE HER!" Rizzo lurched forward, causing his chair to scrape the floor and his cuffs to jangle. His neck muscles went taut, his body rigid, and his face showed real anger. "HOW MANY

TIMES I GOTTA TELL YOU?"

"Maybe a hundred more, or a thousand," Jordan said. "And probably even then, I won't believe you. Believe this, though, Marty: if you don't start providing some answers, you will only dig yourself into a deeper hole. Because the longer it takes to find her, the greater risk that harm comes to that child, and that's all on you. Understand? It's all. On. *You*." She stood, grabbed her notes and file off the table, and tossed Rizzo's cup of water onto the floor. "Oops," she said, and stalked out of the room.

Outside, Jordan leaned against the wall, taking deep breaths. She hadn't broken him—yet. But she would. And until she did, she would make life miserable for Mr. Martin Rizzo.

# Chapter Ten

Preoccupied by everything that had happened that day, Val forgot to press the button in the dorm's elevator. The doors opened on the top level and a pair of young women stared in, waiting for her to exit. She mumbled something about missing her floor and pushed "5," then slid aside to let them in.

Minutes later she unlocked her door on the fifth floor where she shared a room with her longtime friend and confidante, Beth. Val hoped her roomie had waited for her to eat—she had so much to tell her. But she found the room empty, and a quick glance at the clock showed that unless she hustled, she'd miss out on dinner, too. She tossed her backpack onto the bed and headed for the door. Her phone chimed before she locked up.

"Valorie! They have Rizzo!" Rhonda's panicked voice greeted her. "Detective Jordan says if I talk to him, he might reveal Jada's location. But I'm nervous, and I'm not sure what to say. I was wondering..." Her voice trailed off.

Val's stomach rumbled. Soccer practice had left her ravenous, and those sociology chapters wouldn't get read on their own. But then she envisioned Jada, trapped with strangers and afraid, and then imagined her niece, Ali, in the same situation.

Food could wait. Besides, everyone said college women gained fifteen pounds their first semester. She could skip the high-carb offerings at the dining hall without penalty. Maybe she could grab some fruit and yogurt for the road. "Sure," she said. "Pick me up outside my dorm."

"I'm five minutes away," Rhonda said. "Thanks, Val."

They made it to the police station in record time, with Rhonda bubbling over with elation over the prospect of getting her child back. "I've been so worried, I can't even think straight. All I do is eat."

"Lucky you." Val held her empty stomach. "I haven't eaten anything since breakfast."

"So sorry!" Rhonda said. "After we're done at the precinct, I'll buy you dinner. It's the least I can do."

They met a frustrated Detective Jordan in her office, peering into her computer screen. "Bad news," Jordan said. "Rizzo's alibi checks out. His boss and two co-workers verified that he was at work when Jada disappeared."

"But we already knew that a woman grabbed Jada," Val said. "Couldn't he still have masterminded it?"

Jordan laughed. "Interesting choice of words. Rizzo's not smart enough to 'mastermind' tying his own shoes, much less an abduction. Worse, he doesn't even have a permanent residence. We have no clue where to begin looking for the child." Sighing, she circled her desk to face Rhonda. "Still, I think he knows something that will help us, and I hope you can get it from him. Are you up for it?"

"Anything to help find Jada," Rhonda said.

The threesome strategized about how to pry

information out of Rizzo. "Emphasize Jada's safety above all else," Val said, thinking of her own niece. "If he loves her, that ought to sway him."

"If we're lucky, he may still have feelings for you, Rhonda," Jordan said. "Play that up, too. Make him believe it's possible."

Rhonda made a sour face. "Lucky? Not from my point of view," she said. "But I'll try. Can Val be in the room? It'd make me feel a lot more confident, facing him."

"Sorry," Jordan said. "But Val, if you want, you can observe from behind the glass."

"I'd love to!" Val's heart rate spiked. If nothing else, the experience was giving her an amazing inside look at police procedure and strategy.

It also gave her a peek at the lousy diet detectives had to endure. On the way to the interrogation room, she and Detective Jordan bought a quick dinner of granola bars and soft drinks from vending machines in the hall. "Welcome to Café Mansfield," Jordan joked. "Shall I show you our wine list?" She handed Val a grape soda.

But over the course of the next hour, Rizzo refused to budge, insisting that he knew nothing of the abduction, and his story never wavered. The three women gathered back in Jordan's office afterward, all of them glum and dispirited.

"We have diddly-squat on Marty," Jordan said, munching on a Snickers bar. "Other than motive, I mean. No hard evidence. We can hold him on the R.O. violation for a couple of days, but I'm supposed to escort him back to Hartford for that. If we don't come up with something concrete within forty-eight hours, he walks."

"Forty-eight hours! Jada could be long gone, or—or—" Rhonda's face crumpled and she covered it with her hands, bowing her head. Sobs wracked her body.

"It begs the question," Val said, "of who else might have taken the child, if not Rizzo or Desmond."

"Not my brother!" Rhonda said. "Desmond would never do anything to hurt me."

An idea struck Val. "Your brother said some men threatened him in Jamaica," she said. "Did you check Rizzo's phone?"

"No calls to Kingston, or anywhere else down there," Jordan said. "He might have used a burner, but he didn't have one on him, or in his car."

"Let's brainstorm," Val said. "Who else knows about Jada and where Rhonda lives?"

"Asher Mulholland is at the top of that list," Jordan said. "But he also has an alibi, and no motive."

"We must be missing someone," Val said. "Any other relatives? Anyone from one of your classes, or work, or—"

Rhonda sat up in her chair. "There is one person," she said. "Dammit! I can't believe I forgot him."

"Who?" Jordan held her by the shoulders. "I need a name, some details!"

"Sorry I didn't remember him before," Rhonda said. "It just didn't—"

"The name, dammit!" Jordan shouted. "Who is he?"

Rhonda stared wide-eyed, tears running down her cheeks. Her mouth opened, moved as if to form words, but none came, and her head collapsed into her hands again. Jordan fumed and stomped to her desk, cursing under her breath.

Val squatted in front of her friend. An inner voice urged her to rest a hand on Rhonda's knee or shoulder, but something stopped her. Dammit! Once again, her struggles with intimacy and physical touch held her back—this time from connecting with her friend in a moment of need.

But she had other tools.

"Rhonda," she said in a soothing voice. "I'm here to help you. If you can tell me, I can help the detective. Okay?"

Rhonda moaned and leaned over further. "There's a guy," she said, her voice a rough whisper. "We dated one time. His name's Isaac."

"Isaac who?" Val said in a low voice. "How can we find him?"

"Lewis," Rhonda said, regaining control of her voice. "He took me out to dinner once. He got upset with me when I wouldn't go home with him, so he never called me again. I didn't save his number, and he never told me where he lives."

"Got him," Jordan said several minutes later, tapping on her keyboard and staring at her computer. "Or, rather, several guys with that name, but one guy stands out. No phone or current address, though. Has a short rap sheet, including an assault. Does your guy work for an auto dealer in Hartford?"

Rhonda nodded. "He drove a fancy car and claimed it was his. But it had dealer plates and a paper floor mat shoved under the seat."

The detective's printer whirred and spit out a grainy photo image a moment later of a man with light brown skin and curly dark hair.

Val stared at the page in disbelief. "That looks a lot like the guy who chased me today," she said. "Short, kind of stocky build, late 20s?"

"That's him," Rhonda said, sniffling.

Jordan clapped her hands in the air. "Bingo. This guy's a not-nice dude. Hangs around some bad people. People that might try to sell a baby on the open market." She stared up at them. "But ladies, we've got to move. Guys like this don't wait long to fence their goods. Uh, sorry...I mean, they'll want to get Jada into a buyer's hands sooner rather than later. We need to get to her before they do."

# Chapter Eleven

Val recapped the actions of the man who followed her and provided a detailed physical description to Detective Jordan. Then she scanned hundreds of mugshots to identify a more positive match. Isaac Lewis more or less fit the description, but so did a half-dozen other men—including Marty Rizzo.

"That's okay," Jordan said when Val and Rhonda reported back to her office. "We're narrowing the possibilities and adding data. That's detective work, in a nutshell."

"I've never met those other men," Rhonda said. "Why would they take my baby?"

"I'm not saying they would have," Jordan said. "Isaac and Rizzo have connections to you, so they're our top leads. But I'm not counting anyone out."

"Detective," Rhonda said, her voice cracking, "it's been twelve hours since they've taken her. What are the chances she's still in town, and that they haven't..." She couldn't finish. Tears splashed down her face again. Val sat closer, almost even touched her. Almost.

"I'm confident that the people who took her

haven't harmed her," Jordan said. "The longer we go without hearing from them, the less likely it's a ransom situation, and the more likely that they plan to...find her a new home." She paused, then continued in a quiet voice, "As to when they'll move her, it's impossible to say. Once we speak to Mr. Lewis, we may get a better idea of that."

Rhonda's body shook. Val patted her shoulders, but Rhonda batted her arm away. She stood. "I'm sorry," she said. "I need a few minutes. This is all too much." She flung open the door of Jordan's office and rushed through, nearly colliding with Adonna Matthison, her knuckles curled as if to knock.

"Is this a bad time?" Matthison said.

"Come in, Adonna," Jordan said. "What have you found?"

"A bit of good luck, I hope," Matthison said. "Mr. Lewis appears in our system in connection with two other children, each from a different family. In one case, he was tested for paternity—negative. In the other, we interviewed him regarding the temporary disappearance of a foster child of a woman he'd dated. But in that case, the state found the parent at fault for neglect and they moved the child to another home. Mr. Lewis was not implicated."

"How is that good luck?" Val asked. "It seems to exonerate him."

"We have a place of employment, which may be current, and a couple of phone numbers—no longer valid, I'm afraid. It's all in this report." Matthison set a manila folder onto Jordan's desk and cast a wary glance at Val. "Your eyes only, Detective."

Val fumed, but said nothing.

"This is fantastic work," Jordan said. "Just the break we needed. Thank you!" She typed rapid-fire on her keyboard.

"Can I help, somehow?" Val asked.

Jordan paused and frowned. "Sorry, no. This may be a good time for you to find Rhonda and try to console her."

"I'll join you," Matthison said. They exited the detective's office and pulled the door shut.

"So, social work has more in common with detective work than I realized," Val said as they walked, scanning each room as they passed for signs of Rhonda. "Perhaps I've been selling it short."

Matthison smiled. "It can be that way, sometimes," she said. "Tracking down deadbeat dads and sorting out who's causing domestic strife requires some forensic skills. Is social work of interest to you, Ms. Dawes?"

"Let's call it my Plan B," Val said. "My family isn't too happy with my first choice, of becoming a policewoman. Not since my uncle died on the job six years ago."

"How horrible!" Matthison said. "That must have been very traumatic for you. Did you seek counseling?"

They stopped walking and faced each other, Val leaning against the wall for support. "Three years," she said, nodding. "For the first two, we focused on why my mother left a year after my uncle's death. And...well, we talked about a lot of things." She shuddered. The number one topic she'd discussed with her counselor, and the real reason for her therapy, could remain unspoken for now.

*The large man's shadow hovered over
her, his weight crushing her legs, his
breathing ragged. An aroma of alcohol
permeated from his every pore. "Shh," he
said, and continued in a hoarse whisper, "no
one will hear you, anyway. It's just us here
tonight, Valley Girl."*

"You've had some experience with parental
neglect and family dysfunction, then," Matthison
said, shaking her out of the awful memory.

Val nodded, tight-lipped. *Some experience with
parental neglect* might have been the
understatement of the year. Never attentive before
Val's childhood trauma, Mom grew even more
distant over the following year. Then, on that final
gray, rainy day, Mom stood in the doorway,
fumbling with a cigarette and made some excuse
about needing to go visit a friend suffering from
illness. Without so much as a hug goodbye, she
dragged two suitcases to the station wagon and
drove off, never to return.

"Then I can see why social work and helping
families would interest you," Matthison said, again
interrupting her wandering thoughts. "What's the
draw of police work, though? Were you close to
your uncle, perhaps?"

"Very," Val said, her throat tight. "Uncle Val was
my hero, and...well, more than that." *Much more.*
Uncle Val was the only person other than Beth and
her shrink that she'd trusted with the story of what
happened with "Uncle" Milt. But he'd died soon
after, before he could pursue any police action
against her attacker. Val fell silent again and

avoided eye contact with the social worker.

Fortunately, Rhonda emerged from the ladies' room behind Matthison a moment later, her eyes red, her face still wet with tears. "I'm sorry for running out on you all," she said. "What did I miss?"

"I'd like to speak with you, if I could," Matthison said to Rhonda. "Ms. Dawes, would you excuse us?"

"Of course." Val sighed. Again, Matthison was cutting her out of the conversation. Val's silent frustration grew as Rhonda and Adonna ducked into a meeting room, closing the door behind them.

Val shuffled down the hall, not knowing where it would lead her, or what she should do with herself. She returned to the small conference room she'd used before and sat at the table, facing out. A few officers and clerks glanced at her as they shuffled past, but said nothing, apparently satisfied that she had a reason for being there.

Which she didn't. But she didn't know what else to do. She should do something, but what?

A moment later she answered her own question. She'd do what she excelled at, besides sports: research.

Val pulled her laptop out of her backpack and opened her browser. She searched the web for tidbits on Isaac Lewis, finding dozens of items on other men with his name—no help. She added to the search: "Isaac+Lewis+baby." Several birth announcements filled her screen. No good. She recalled Adonna's stories and entered a new search: "Isaac+Lewis+foster+child." This time, a short news article popped up, which she guessed related to the episode Adonna had described, near the airport in Windsor Locks. That caught her attention: a baby trafficker might want easy access to national and international flights. A second article connected him to a carjacking case in Hartford—as a witness, rather than a suspect. A third mentioned his arrest as a bit player in a money-laundering case, also in Hartford. He'd turned state's evidence in a plea deal that kept him out of prison.

And, potentially, put him in debt to some terrible people.

She navigated to another site, one that claimed to provide "secret" information about anyone and everyone...for a fee. She typed in his name, producing a list of potential candidates. One listed an Isaac Lewis who worked as a driver for an auto repair chain headquartered in Hartford. That matched what Rhonda knew of him. After she clicked on the link, the screen demanded payment of $59.95 for a "full report." The report promised his home address, employer information, his phone number, and a slew of data irrelevant to her needs, like his credit score. But the rest would be useful.

She considered it. Was it worth sixty bucks to obtain her own leads? Child Services had nothing like this. No doubt Tanisha Jordan had access to similar information, but she'd decided not to share. Val felt useless, unable to help. With information on Isaac, she might make a difference.

But she had a problem. Paying for tuition, books, room, and board had drained her bank account. Her father had promised to replenish it on his next payday, another week from Friday. In the meantime, he'd supplied her with a Visa card and admonished her to use it "only in emergencies." He'd spelled out what constituted an emergency: things like food, can't-wait school supplies, a late-night taxi home, and posting bail made the list. Alcohol, football tickets, and online data searches had not. "Anything else," he'd warned her, "check with me first."

Still. Dad couldn't have anticipated this. "Better to ask forgiveness than permission," Uncle Val had always said.

She whipped out her dad's credit card and typed in the number. Moments later, she knew how to find Isaac Lewis.

# Chapter Twelve

Val's discoveries got her excited, but the constant traffic of officers past the meeting room jangled her nerves. If Jordan caught wind of her efforts, she might shut Val out of the investigation, and then she would be no help at all to Rhonda. After a half hour of furtive research, she packed up her laptop and scheduled a ride-share back to campus. Pangs of guilt stabbed at Val's stomach when she left without saying goodbye to Rhonda. But she and Adonna Matthison were still talking when Val strolled past their closed door, and she didn't want to interrupt.

Distracted, she got no studying done that night and even less sleeping. She'd hoped to share the long day's adventures with her roommate, but Beth had left a note on Val's bed, saying she had a date. The "date" apparently included breakfast, as Beth's bed remained empty and undisturbed when Val gave up on getting any shuteye in the morning. Bleary-eyed, she trudged down the stairs to the dorm lobby, hoping to grab a quick oatmeal and coffee in the dining hall before her 9 a.m. English composition class.

Before Val made it twenty feet out of the building, an angry Rhonda LeMieux blocked her path, arms crossed.

"You have a lot of nerve!" Rhonda shouted.

Val froze in mid-stride, and the backpack slung over her shoulder bounced against her arm. "Excuse me?" she said. "What are you doing here?"

"You can't hide from me!" Rhonda yelled. "You sneaky little bitch!" She shoved Val backwards, hard.

Without thinking, Val's jiu jitsu training kicked in. Reacting to the push, her body flew into a defensive posture: crouched, feet spread to shoulder width, arms level, and fingers curled into a tight fist. The pose lasted only a second before she relaxed again, but not before surprise registered on her friend's face.

"You're going to hit me?" she said. "It's not enough that you lied about me to Child Services. You want to put me into the hospital, too?"

"What are you talking about?" Val searched Rhonda's face for clues, but found only anger. "What's that about Child Services?"

"Don't play innocent with me," Rhonda said, seething. "Right after your secret chat with her, Ms. Matthison told me her research revealed a 'pattern of neglect' in my care for Jada. What did you tell her?" Rhonda shoved Val again, tears staining her cheeks. "I could lose my girl, even after I get her back!"

"I said no such thing," Val said, "to her or anyone else. I don't know anything about your parenting practices, but if I did—"

"See? That's what I'm talking about!" Rhonda fumed and paced in circles in front of Val. "I'd hoped you had my back, but you went spreading lies to the cops and the state and everybody. You say you want to help, but all the while you're stabbing me in the back. Well, Miss Valorie Dawes, I don't need friends like you. Stay the hell away from me! Do you hear me? Keep away!" Rhonda glared and pointed a long finger in Val's face, then stalked off, her feet stomping on the pavement.

Val gazed after Rhonda, her jaw dropping. She hadn't discussed Rhonda's parenting practices with Child Services. However, somebody else clearly had.

But who? And, more important, why?

*** 

The confrontation with Rhonda left Val shaken, and feeling like an idiot for thinking she could somehow help her friend. Danger aside, devoting precious study hours to helping someone who didn't appreciate or want it seemed foolish now.

The argument had left her even less time for breakfast. She grabbed a yogurt and coffee-to-go from the dining hall and hurried toward campus. If she hustled, she could make it to the English Department building with enough time to review her essay on the virtues of competitive sports before handing it in.

And she *would* have made it on time had Detective Tanisha Jordan not greeted her at the front door, hand raised high, signaling her to stop.

"I need to talk to you further about the man who followed you yesterday evening," Jordan said. "Can you come downtown with me?"

"I have class," Val said. "Which you know, apparently, since you're here. How did you find me?"

Jordan smiled. "I'd be a lousy college-town cop if I couldn't navigate my way through a university bureaucracy," she said. "That, and my sister works for the registrar."

Val peeked around her, spotting her professor climbing the steps to enter the building. "Let me turn in my paper and get the next assignment," she said. "It won't take 15 minutes."

Jordan nodded and waved Val inside. "Hurry," she said.

Val caught up with her English teacher in the hallway. He grumped about giving her "special treatment," but relented when she filled him in on the details of the case. "Email me for today's assignment," he said. "You'll need to borrow notes on the lecture from a fellow student."

She thanked him and found Jordan waiting by her blue Dodge Charger, parked in a tow-away zone in front of the building. "Nobody will tow a cop," Jordan said, grinning. "Not twice, anyway."

"I guess there are a few nice perks of the profession," Val said. "Good to know. Lately, the only things I've heard about becoming a cop have been negative."

Jordan shot her a sideways glance. "Sorry if my comments yesterday discouraged you," she said. "That wasn't my intention."

Val sighed. "My professor, Dr. Hirsch says police work is a 'man's job.' Dangerous, physical, and tough. Did I mention he's a sexist jerk?"

"No need," Jordan said, grinning. "I had Hirsch for Crim 101 eighteen years ago. From what people tell me, he's softened up some."

"How is that possible?" Val said, but she laughed along with the detective. "He makes Neanderthal men seem like Barack Obama."

"Sounds like Horrible Hirsch to me," Jordan

said, her laughter fading into a wry smile. "And he's *mostly* wrong, but right enough to justify his point of view to himself."

"Which part is he right about?" Val asked. "If you don't mind my asking."

Jordan grimaced. "He's correct that it's physically demanding, dangerous, and tough, but not that males are any more suited to handling it than females," she said. "Men are bigger weenies than women in a lot of ways. Zero pain tolerance, fragile egos, no patience—and those are the good ones."

"Sounds like a gross over-generalization," Val said. "My uncle had the patience of Job, and I saw no sign of an ego. He also lived through two shootings..." Her throat tightened, and tears formed in the corners of her eyes. "Not the third one, though," she said, her voice raspy. Her heart doubled in size, or so it felt. No room in her chest for lungs, or air to fill them, suddenly.

"Your uncle was a king among men," Jordan said. "But you're right. I'm being a little harsh on the guys. That's because they're tough on me, and they'll be tough on you, too."

"How so?" Val asked.

Jordan grimaced again. "Hirsch is right that women have it tough in law enforcement, but for the wrong reasons," she said. "Guys don't have to put up with men coming on to them, grabbing their asses, and laughing it all off as 'a joke.' Men accept each other's presence in the squad car, but they're uncomfortable with ours—and again, I'm talking about the good ones. Bad ones are resentful, sometimes hostile. The worst among them won't partner with us. The old guard in management—

which isn't everyone, but it's enough of them—pass women over for opportunities that lead to promotions. They'll say they're doing us a favor, keeping us out of harm's way. Then when that sergeant exam comes up and your experiences don't measure up to theirs, they shrug and say, 'You just don't have the resume.' But they never acknowledge their role in that process."

Val exhaled a loud breath. "Wow. Sounds like the old glass ceiling has multiple layers of acrylic piled on top."

"And alligators," Jordan said, laughing. "And laser beams. But it's not all bad. Sure, opportunities for women are limited. However, when they open up, it's often easier for individual women to win them because of how few of us there are. Supply and demand, and all that."

"You mean, for affirmative-action hires, for example? 'We need to promote a woman this month' sort of thing?" Val asked.

Jordan nodded. "You're quick on the uptake, Dawes." She smiled. "You'll make a good detective someday."

Val's ears reddened, but her heart swelled. "Thanks," she said. "It's what I've always wanted to do. Until lately, that is. I've started to doubt myself, now that I've heard some of these stories."

Jordan parked in the lot behind the precinct station. "No knocks on your college education, but nothing beats experience," she said.

An idea took shape in Val's mind. "Say," she said. "I was wondering. Would it be possible for me to follow you around for a few hours sometime to watch what your typical day is like? I promise, I won't interfere with anything. I just want to learn."

Jordan parked and eyed her with caution. "You want to shadow me, eh?" She gazed out the front windshield. "There's a public outreach program where citizens can ride along in squad cars, but that's reserved for patrol units. You're looking for a more practical, up-close-and-personal experience, am I right?"

"Something like that," Val said. "I'll check into that ride-along thing. But I thought if I shadowed you, I'd see the daily life of a detective—and what it's like for a woman. That's a lot more relevant for me."

"I can see that," Jordan said. "Now, you'd have to keep your yap shut. No butting in, ever. No talking out of school, either, so to speak."

"Never," Val said. "Girls' honor."

Jordan grinned at her. "Okay, Dawes. We'll do that. In fact, I was thinking of something along those lines myself, believe it or not."

"You were?" Val said, excitement building. "That's awesome! Thank you!"

"On that note," Jordan said, "let's talk about Isaac Lewis."

# Chapter Thirteen

Tanisha Jordan noticed Dawes startle at the second mention of Isaac Lewis. Val had steered the conversation away from him and onto her interest in the life of a female cop, and seemed...what? Upset wasn't quite the word. Unnerved, perhaps. Surprised, at least. As if, by changing the subject, Dawes counted on Jordan forgetting about her main objective in picking Dawes up that morning.

Not frigging likely, as her father used to say when he thought the kids were out of earshot. She'd become a detective because of her tenacity and laser-like focus. Dozens of career criminals far more capable of avoiding tough interrogation had preceded Dawes in similar attempts. None had derailed her investigations.

"When Isaac Lewis followed you last evening," Jordan said when they'd reached her office, "would you characterize it as him trying to isolate or intimidate you? Or was it more like following you to, say, see where you lived or who you might be meeting?"

Dawes gnawed on her lower lip. "I couldn't tell," she said. "He tried to stay hidden at first, but once

I picked up the pace, he did his best to close the gap. Another hundred yards and he might have."

"With your track speed?" Jordan said. "Couldn't you outrun him?"

"I was exhausted...from soccer practice." Her voice lacked its usual clarity and conviction, however. As if Dawes didn't believe her own words.

Jordan leaned in and lowered her voice. "Ms. Dawes," Jordan said, "were you trying to let him catch you?"

"No!" Dawes reacted as if the detective had slapped her. "I thought it was Rizzo, remember? The guy who abducted Jada."

"It might have been the kidnapper," Jordan said. "Just not Rizzo."

"Why would he come after me?" Dawes asked. "How would that help them?"

Jordan nodded, leaned back, and drew a deep breath. "It seems strange that they haven't contacted her, and yet, there's also no sign of the child in any of the usual channels," she said. "That tells me they're being especially cautious, and not just because they've realized she's gone to the police. It confirms that she knows these people, rather than it being some random kidnapper. They're aware that she's looking, and has help. Besides the police." She fixed her gaze on Dawes, waited for the logical conclusion to dawn on her. It only took a moment.

"That's right," Jordan said. "You. They're watching her, so they know you're in the picture. They've probably figured out who you are. Who your uncle was. And if they conclude that you're anything like him, then you're trouble—and they want you out of the way."

Dawes sat up straighter, growing more animated—as if she relished this revelation. "Could they have gotten to Adonna Matthison somehow?" she asked.

Jordan's mouth hung open. Of all the responses, that was perhaps the one she least expected. "Why do you ask?"

"Someone fed Ms. Matthison some misinformation, apparently, and Rhonda accused me," she said. "If they're trying to isolate her, and discovered the case involved Child Services—"

"Isaac Lewis would know that," Jordan said. "As would Rizzo. They're both in the system, and both know how it works. So it doesn't eliminate either from suspicion, but makes them both more likely than anyone else."

"Wouldn't Desmond LeMieux also realize that?" Dawes asked in a dull voice, as if uttering the words pained her.

A chill swept across Jordan's brow. "Yes, he would," she said. "Okay, that makes three strong suspects. Although I don't see a strong motive for the brother."

"I agree," Dawes said. "But one of the other guys might've threatened him somehow, made him an unwilling accomplice." She made a face. "I didn't sense that from him, though. Desmond seemed afraid, yes, but also surprised by the whole thing."

Jordan considered this. Her skeptical nature pushed her toward suspecting everyone, but Dawes had shown intelligence and strong instincts. Enough to make her rethink things, if only a little. "Well, he's Jamaica's problem, for now," she said. "They've kept an eye on him and haven't spotted him meeting with anyone suspicious. Regardless, I've got to focus on what I can do here. Which brings me to my proposition." She lowered her voice again. "I'd like you to help me."

Dawes practically danced in her chair, grinning. "I'd love to!" she said. "What can I do?"

"Don't say yes just yet," Jordan said, her heart pounding. Her plan carried significant risks—for Dawes, herself, the department, and perhaps most important, for Jada. "If I'm right, they're likely to follow you again—and this time, make contact. I want us to be ready."

"That makes perfect sense," Dawes said. "What does that entail?"

Jordan surrendered a wan smile. "How do you feel," she asked, "about setting yourself up as bait?"

The sparkle in Dawes's eyes gave Jordan all the answer she needed.

***

The operation Jordan suggested required approval of higher-ups and would take a few hours to set up. In the meantime, Val returned to campus for her 11:00 a.m. Spanish class. However, she hadn't studied for the lesson, and couldn't keep up with the instructor's rapid-fire grammar and vocabulary drills. Not that she could have focused on it, anyway. Nothing could drive the worry about Jada from her mind—nor her excitement over Detective Jordan's dangerous but enticing proposal.

Jordan's strategy required Val to remain as visible as possible. She would continue to attend classes and soccer practice, eat at the dining hall, and study outdoors during the gaps in between. Jordan assigned a plain clothes patrol officer to follow her at a distance, ready to call in backup at a moment's notice. Still, she'd remain at risk for at least a short while, particularly if Isaac, or whoever, spotted Val first. To stay safe during those brief moments, Val would rely on her own wits and athleticism.

She felt good about that.

Val remained so absorbed in her thoughts that the other students had cleared the room before she realized that class was over.

"*Sigues dormido, Señorita* Dawes?" the instructor said with a grin as she gathered up her teaching materials. When Val responded with a blank stare, the instructor added, "Shall I set a wake-up alarm for you?"

"Sorry," Val said, stuffing books into her backpack. "I...have a lot going on."

"Perhaps by Friday," the teacher said, her grin disappearing, "Spanish vocabulary will be going on, no?" She hurried out of the room, speeding through a group of students already pushing their way in to assume their seats for the next class.

Val stumbled past them moments later and entered the bright sunshine of the hot summer afternoon, shading her eyes with her hand—she'd forgotten to bring sunglasses. After strolling to the dining hall, she took her lunch outside, munching a dry sandwich under the shade of an oak tree, keeping her eyes peeled for Isaac. No sign of him, or anyone suspicious-looking. She pulled her Spanish textbook out of her backpack and spread it open on her lap. With the little free time remaining before soccer practice, she might as well catch up on her studies.

Ten minutes later, she woke with a start, propped up against the tree trunk, the book open to a random, wind-blown page. Too many carbs, too much hot sun. Studies might need to wait. Besides, there was something else she needed to do.

She found her friend's name in her contacts list and dialed.

Voice-mail.

"Rhonda," she said, "I wanted to talk to you about this whole Child Services thing. Detective Jordan may have figured out who's feeding her that bad information about you. Also, I was hoping we could talk about our Crim—oh, wait. Is that you calling me?" She checked Caller ID. Sure enough, "Rhonda LeMieux—Mobile" appeared on her screen. She switched to the live call. "Rhonda! Thanks for calling me back. I was just—"

"Wait, please," Rhonda said. "I want to say something to you first."

Val paused, her spirits lifting. No doubt she'd calmed down since the night before and reconsidered things. "No need to apologize," Val said. "It's all good. Things like this happen."

"Apologize?" Rhonda's voice betrayed surprise and anger, magnified by her Island accent. "Why would I apologize to *you*?"

"Uh...I'm sorry," Val said. "I assumed that you—"

"You assume a lot, all the time!" Rhonda shouted. "Like what you know about me and what it means to be my friend. You've got some nerve, girl!"

Stunned, Val found herself unable to speak.

Only a tiny choke emerged from her mouth.

"What I was calling to say is," Rhonda said, "it's best if we find other partners for our group project. Considering what's happened."

Another few seconds passed before Val could respond. "Okay, sure," she said. "If that's how you feel."

"Keep the 'Women in Crime' topic," Rhonda said. "I'll pick something else. Okay, that's all I wanted to say. Goodbye."

"Rhonda, wait! I have something—"

But the line had already gone dead.

\*\*\*

The damned. Kid. Wouldn't. Stop. *Crying.*

The squat, curly-haired man sat on the bed and covered his ears, pressing so tight he gave himself a headache. Even through two closed bedroom doors twenty feet apart, the kid's high-pitched wail pierced his eardrums and shattered his concentration. He hadn't slept in over 48 hours, which only made things worse.

"Shut that damned kid *up!*" he yelled.

The woman responded with a slew of muffled Creole invective. At least, he assumed so from her tone. He didn't understand a word of it.

Still, he had to show her who was in charge. "Spare me the damned excuses!" he yelled at her. "Just make her stop crying!"

More high-speed Creole, even less comprehensible than before. The crying continued.

The man could take no more. He pounded across the apartment, his anger growing. The volume of the kid's screams doubled. He pushed the door open to the kid's room.

The woman flew by him, hands in the air, still cursing in Creole. A few of the words he understood, and his anger intensified. How dare she call him that! He followed, raging at her. "Where the hell are you going? How are you going to shut that brat up from down here?"

Pounding on the front door startled him. "Hey, keep it down in there!" a guy yelled from the corridor outside.

The woman shouted something and raced to the door. That bitch! If she let the guy in, he'd be done for. Catching up to her, he grabbed her arm and yanked her back. She screamed. Like, *loud.* Like bloody murder loud.

"What's going on in there?" the guy in the hall yelled. "Ma'am, are you in trouble? Open up, or I'm calling the cops!"

The woman's eyes met his, and they both froze. Good—she understood the situation. Maybe she'd shut up for a half-second and do something about the kid.

Her lips pursed, and a gob of wet, gooey spit landed on his face.

With his free hand, he wiped his face, but the Creole bitch chose that moment to shove him, and he tumbled backward, losing his grip on her arm. His full weight crashed onto the cheap wooden coffee table, smashing it to pieces. She yanked on the door handle. Two deadbolts stopped her. She wrestled with them, her movements rushed and awkward.

Squat Man lunged for the woman, got his arms wrapped around her knees, and her body smashed into the wall. A loud "oof!" escaped her lips and she swore at  him again.

"Who's in there?" the guy in the hall shouted. "You got illegals in there? I swear, if this door doesn't open in five seconds, I'm calling Homeland Security!"

"*Imigrasyon! Merde!*" the woman said through clenched teeth. "*Retire men ou, estipid!*"

"You're not going anywhere," Squat said. "Just zip your lip. And shut that kid up, too!"

"That's it, I'm calling the feds," Hall Guy said. "You're going to prison, jerk-off. I promise you that!" Footsteps pounded in the corridor, followed by a slamming door.

The squat man struggled to his feet, but a sharp pain in the shape of a foot split his buttocks. He howled and spun to face her. Mistake! A second kick crushed his testicles, and he sank to his knees, eyes watering. The woman unbolted the door and flew into the hallway, spewing more unintelligible Creole invective.

He got her meaning, however. The woman was leaving and not coming back. He was stuck with a kid who never stopped crying, who probably needed her damned diaper changed, and food, and God knows what else. He had no idea how to take care of a child and didn't care to learn.

But he couldn't stay in the apartment—not with federal agents coming to haul the immigrant woman back to wherever she'd come from. And he couldn't leave behind the crying brat—his meal ticket. He'd have to take her along and force his buyer's hand.

They wouldn't budge, however, until he got rid of the mother and her meddlesome friend.

A new idea formed in his mind. One that, he realized, would solve both problems.

# Chapter Fourteen

The day grew blisteringly hot, and Val returned to her dorm room to change into shorts and a T-shirt. She loaded up her backpack for 3:00 soccer practice and headed back toward campus. She again took the back route between the chapels, across the cemetery, and down the steps among the cluster of science buildings. With over an hour to spare, she considered sprawling out on the green next to the Engineering building.

Val had just picked out a shady spot under a tree when a short, squat man appeared in the reflection of the windows of the Student Union.

*Isaac!*

Val checked her first impulse—*Run!* Jordan had prepared her for this, when fear triggered her survival instinct. But she followed the detective's advice from that morning: *Pause. Take a deep breath. Act as if nothing is wrong.*

Glancing around, she spotted a bike rack and pretended to inspect one of the sturdy Schwinns locked to the metal frame. She kept her eye on Isaac's reflection until he moved out of view, calculating his position while resisting the impulse to stare in his direction.

Then she realized: *he didn't have the baby.*

Of course not, she scolded herself. Only an idiot would bring Jada along in public. But then, where had he left her?

She pretended to answer her phone, instead sending a brief text to Detective Jordan, and resumed her progress toward the sports complex. That meant moving closer to Isaac, but with the crowd of students bustling past in every direction, she felt safe from attack. Still, it took effort to resist the urge to press the button on another one of those blue emergency call towers as she passed. They needed to lure him in, not scare him away.

Sweat dripped down her back and shone on her arms. The day's humidity made her breathing labored while she walked, even with the great shape she kept herself in. At the intersection she veered right, circling around the basketball pavilion where she'd first spotted him the day before. She crossed the street to take advantage of the shaded walkway along the campus bookstore. That, she hoped, would allow her to use the reflections in the building's glass front to track Isaac's movements. But that proved difficult with him trailing her. She stole a single glance over her shoulder, too quick to locate him in the broad array of windows. After facing forward again, a familiar voice interrupted her.

"Dawes! Wait up a sec!" The lanky figure of Robb McFarland stepped into her path, wearing a polo shirt, chino shorts, and a lazy smile. "Hey, I was just noticing that you hadn't signed up for a research topic in Sociology, and your friend Rhonda chose a different partner. Any chance I can talk you into teaming up with me?"

Val's gut turned, this time from exasperation rather than fear. "I don't know," she said. "I'm kind of busy right now, though. Can't we chat later?"

"You don't look busy to me," he said. "Anyway, the deadline for signing up is three o'clock today. From what I can tell, you and I are the only ones who haven't chosen topics and partners."

Val sighed. She'd hoped to convince Rhonda to change her mind. But if her friend had signed up with someone else already, Val might have no choice but to partner with the insufferable McFarland. "What topics do we have left to choose from?" she asked.

"Lots. That women-in-crime thing, for example. Which is kind of boring, if you ask me, but—"

"I didn't," she said. "Listen, I have to get going." She strode down the sidewalk, stealing a glance in the reflection, again failing to spot Isaac. McFarland tagged along, keeping up with long strides and barely breaking a sweat.

"You really ought to consider my offer, Dawes. I don't often give second chances," he said. "But you've made a name for yourself, and you're obviously smart for a woman, so—"

"Get the hell away from me," she said, her tone half as sharp as she intended. Isaac remained at the top of her mind, diluting her frustration with McFarland. Plus, with Robb hanging by her side, Isaac might give up the chase, and she'd lose the opportunity to catch him quickly—and find Jada. "I don't have time for this."

"I'm happy to choose another topic," he said, huffing a little as he tried to keep up. "Maybe 'Poverty and Race as Predictors of Crime'? Or how about—"

"Do whatever you want," Val said, quickening her pace. Guy could not take a hint.

"I'll take that as meaning I should sign up for both of us." Robb paused on the sidewalk. "How about we meet tonight at seven to go over our outline?"

Val shook her head, gazing up at the heavens and letting out a loud growl. Maybe she should drag him along. Knock him out, trade him to Isaac for the baby. His family had money. Surely he presented a more lucrative target.

"Text me your digits!" Robb shouted after her.

She sighed. So much for that plan. Nobody would pay a ransom for that idiot. Checking the reflections again, she spotted Isaac across the street, near the pavilion, still tagging along. Good. She faced forward and maintained a steady pace toward the athletic complex.

Her phone buzzed. Text message from Jordan: "Location?"

Val replied: "UC bkstr 2 scr fld." Kept walking.

"Isaac?" came the reply.

"Y. On ft." Val lost the shaded area of sidewalk and squinted into the sun.

"Be there in 5," Jordan texted back. Still nothing from Rhonda.

Val reached the end of the parking garage and crossed to Isaac's side of the street, toward the rear door of the natatorium. As she turned, she glimpsed Isaac, still following. Closer than expected—maybe only forty yards away—but distant enough that she could escape if needed.

"Dawes!"

Val turned. Her frustration reached the boiling

point when she spied Robb McFarland, once again trailing behind.

"Robb!" she shouted. "Leave me alone right now. Please!"

"It'll only take a second," he said, turning on what passed for charm on his planet. "I need your student ID number to 'prove' that we're research partners on Professor Hirsch's website." McFarland smiled and held up his phone, as if she could read it from twenty feet away.

"Oh, for heaven's sake!" Her shoulders sagged. "Can't we do this later?"

"Then we'd miss the deadline," he said. "I can't afford anything less than an 'A' in this class. Come on, Dawes. Be a sport."

Val rolled her eyes and scanned the horizon over his shoulder. No sign of Isaac. "Okay, here." She met him halfway and held out her student ID. Robb tapped it into his phone and grinned. "Excellent! All set. I'm so looking forward to this. You won't regret this, Dawes."

"I already do," she said in a low voice. "Now, please, excuse me. I need to change for soccer practice, or I'll be late."

Robb shaded his eyes and peered over her shoulder. "I don't see any of your teammates out there," he said. "Are you sure you have practice today, in this heat?"

"I'm sure!" She regretted the sharpness in her tone...a little. Her irritation had more to do with the possibility of spooking Isaac than with Robb's annoying personality. "Now, please?..."

He cocked his head and smirked. "Am I stopping you, for reals?" He winked at her. "Or are you waiting for, say, an invitation to dinner? Because I could totally make that work—"

"Good-bye, Robb." Turning away, she spotted Isaac, peeking around the corner of the building.

"You know," Robb said, "I don't have a lot going on right now. Mind if I stay and watch you practice?"

"Yes, I mind!" This time she intended the forceful tone. "Please. Go. Away!"

Robb's sly smile faded and he raised his hands in surrender. "Okay, okay. Jeez, you can't blame a guy for trying." He drifted away, keeping his eye on her for the first few seconds, then faced forward and traipsed off with a slight spring in his step.

Val headed toward the clubhouse entrance, but stopped at the door and slid back along the wall to the corner, listening for footsteps. Nothing. Had she scared Isaac off? Doubtful. She searched for Jordan's Dodge Charger or a Mansfield police cruiser. None.

Sweat trickled down her face. She had to keep Isaac close, but not too close, until backup arrived. On this side of the building, nobody else lingered. Even the parking lot remained empty of people. She had to move.

In a moment, she found her solution. A red track circled the soccer field. She could run a few laps before practice. Slow ones, in this heat. Coach Hillebrand might think her crazy, but it would keep Val on the move, and Isaac close, and provide enough time for Jordan to arrive.

With a final glance Isaac's way, she trotted toward the field.

\*\*\*

Isaac followed the young woman, staying close

to the side of the building—an arena or practice facility, he couldn't tell which. The closest he'd ever come to college sports had been watching basketball on TV. The amount of money spent on these athletes—

He shook his head. Can't get distracted now. Focus on getting this woman alone, then take her out. Permanently. And fast. He'd left the kid unguarded for several minutes now. Can't risk much longer. That made him sweat even more than the near-100-degree heat and humidity.

He peeked around the corner. The woman had company! Some skinny, pasty-faced white boy— from the looks of him, a rich kid. The kind that never seem to sweat, no matter how hot the day got. Had nothing to worry about, those kids. Everything handed to them. Never had to fight, to scrape, to take crazy chances and risk prison or death to keep from starving to death.

She looked Isaac's way, and he ducked back out of her view. A few guys walking out of the facility's front door stopped and stared at him. Isaac pretended to respond to a text message on his phone. After several seconds the men shrugged and walked on. Clusters of students across the street paid him no mind at all. But this street was far too busy. Somehow he had to maneuver her into a more secluded spot.

Like, the lot next to the field, where he'd parked his car.

The skinny kid ambled past, his nose buried in his cell phone. Took forever, but he finally turned and headed back toward the center of campus. Good. She'd be alone now.

He braved another peek around the building.

Sure enough, she trotted, unaccompanied, toward the soccer field, empty except for a few idiots braving the heat, jogging around the track. But that put her out in the open, where anyone could see her—and him, if he approached her. He'd need to get to her before she reached the gate, without attracting too much attention. But how?

He slid around the building and along the wall as fast as he dared, losing ground with every step. He needed to keep her outside those gates. Then he remembered: the Porsche he'd "borrowed" from the dealership had one of those remote key fobs with the built-in panic alarm. He fished it out of his pocket and pressed the red button. He hoped it would pick up the signal at this distance—he'd left it in the shade at the far end of the lot.

The vehicle's lights flashed, its horn blaring. The woman paused to look. He had to hurry—she wouldn't stop for long.

But he was wrong about that.

\*\*\*

The blaring horn blasted Val out of her obsession with Isaac, and she halted her jog to determine where it was coming from. She spotted the vehicle, a fancy sports car, in the rear corner of the lot next to the soccer complex. Not a gold Toyota, like the kidnapper drove.

She sighed, a nervous release of tension. This car probably belonged to some spoiled brat—Robb McFarland, for example. No doubt Robb had pressed his panic button by accident, or forgot where he parked and didn't care that his method of finding it disturbed others. She turned back toward the field, but stopped when another noise trickled in between horn blasts.

The sound of a baby crying.

Or, to be more precise, a toddler.

The realization hit her like the charge of an angry midfielder: the car was Isaac's, not Robb's. And the child was Jada!

Val broke into a run, heading toward the Porsche, her lungs heaving out steamy air with every step. The heat provoked even more rage and fear: the idiot Isaac had locked Jada inside on a 95-degree day, for God knows how long. He could have killed her!

Footsteps pounded somewhere behind her. Good—she'd have help. As she ran, she slid her backpack off her shoulders and unzipped it. The action slowed her down, but enabled her to search the bag for something to break into the car with. But its contents provided nothing of use: her soccer clothes, cleats, laptop, and a Spanish textbook. Nothing hard enough to smash windows or sharp enough to pick the lock.

She reached the Porsche, its horn blaring and lights flashing. The driver—presumably, Isaac—had left the windows rolled down an inch or two. The tinted glass made it tough to see inside, so Val peeked in through the cracks.

Sure enough, a toddler sat in the back. No child safety seat, just strapped into the seat belt, crying at the top of her lungs. Val recognized the girl from the picture. No doubt at all: it was Jada.

Footsteps thudded closer. Not wanting to take her eyes off Jada, Val shouted over her shoulder to the oncoming runner. "Help me get into this car. There's a child inside!" She gripped the window with both hands and tried to push it down. It wouldn't budge. She shook it, hoping to snap it off. No luck. She banged on it with her fists, then with her Spanish text, to no avail. She turned to plead for help.

The blow landed on her temple, and in a flash of pain, she crumpled in a heap on the pavement.

# Chapter Fifteen

Tanisha Jordan arrived at Parking Lot D, outside of the UConn soccer practice facility, expecting to find Valorie Dawes somewhere in the vicinity. Maybe not in the lot, but perhaps on the field, or running laps on the track. Worst case, she'd be findable by phone or text. Dawes was young, but reliable. Not a quitter or a flake who'd freak out and bail at the first sign of trouble.

Jordan drove a snail's pace, scanning the field at the same time. Nobody out there, and who could blame them, in this heat? She reached the end of the lot and turned to circle around. She stopped short when a skinny white kid in a polo shirt and shorts ran in front of her car.

"Watch out!" she yelled. Wasted effort, with her windows up and the AC on. She lowered the driver's side window and leaned into the wall of heat that greeted her. "You crazy, mister?" she called to the boy. "You trying to get killed?"

"Sorry!" The kid looked worried, and not just from the close call.

The radio blasted a cacophony of static, reporting a burglary in progress across town. She turned it down.

"Are you a policeman?" the kid asked. "Er, police *woman*. Sorry."

She badged him. "Detective Jordan, Mansfield P.D. You in trouble, son?"

The kid scurried closer, leaned on her car door. "That Porsche that just left? I think he took my friend!"

"What Porsche? Who's your friend?" Alarm bells rang in her head. According to reports, Isaac worked for a car dealer and liked to show off by driving the fanciest ride in the fleet.

"Valorie—"

"*Dawes?*"

The kid nodded, surprise plastered across his face. "You know her?"

"Hop in!" Jordan unlocked her passenger door, attached her portable flashers to the roof, and switched them on. "Did you get a license plate? Description? Anything? Hell, kid, what's *your* name?"

"Robbin McFarland," he said, buckling his seat belt. He bounced back in his seat when Jordan floored the gas pedal, burning rubber out of the parking lot. "The car was a silver Porsche Carrera. Pretty new—2013 or '14. Connecticut dealer plates, but I didn't get the numbers."

"You know cars?" Jordan honked her horn and zoomed around the slow-moving traffic.

"My dad has one like it, in green. The Porsche turned right, by the way."

Jordan nodded and accelerated around the curve, blasting her horn to clear the campus streets of clueless pedestrians. A few, wearing headphones, seemed oblivious even to the crazy amount of noise she was generating, but she got past them without losing too much speed. "Did you get a look at the guy?"

"The driver?" McFarland said. "Not really. Kind of short and chunky, with dark hair. I didn't see his face."

Jordan grimaced. Could be Isaac or Rizzo. "S'awright. We'll find him. How many Porsches can there be with a captive female student inside?"

The kid frowned. "Maybe a half dozen," he said. To her startled reaction, he added, "This *is* a college campus, after all."

"Okay, I'll give you that." Jordan radioed in the description to dispatch. At the edge of campus, she rolled through the turn onto Route 275, heading west, and floored it again.

"How do you know where you're going?" Robb held on for dear life and his skin looked even whiter, somehow.

She grunted. "I have an idea who we're after and where he lives," she said. Right or wrong, it at least gave her a place to go.

"Are you sure I should be in here with you?" Robb asked. His complexion had already changed from pasty white to a sickly green.

"If you puke, do it out the window," she said. "What else? Did you see him take her?"

McFarland clenched his eyes shut as she zoomed past a truck in a no-passing zone. "She approached the Porsche and yelled something about a baby inside," he said. "The fat guy slapped her or punched her, and she fell. When I called out, she didn't answer. I walked toward them, but I was at least a hundred yards away. The next thing I know, the Porsche is racing past me, and when I got to the spot where he hit her, she was gone."

"So you're not *certain* that he took her."

"Where else would she be?" He opened his eyes and shook his head in disbelief.

"Okay, okay. You mentioned something about a baby?" She reached the open road and stomped on the gas.

Robb nodded and squeezed his eyes shut again. "Apparently it was locked inside the car. On a hot day like this—"

The radio blasted again. "Suspect vehicle spotted traveling northbound at high speed on Stafford Road, near the Middle Turnpike," the dispatcher said. "Patrol vehicles en route."

"Copy." Jordan glanced at McFarland, his skin as green as a Granny Smith apple. He was right— she couldn't take him with her. "I'll drop you off at the next intersection, at the fire station," she said. "A patrol car will pick you up. We'll want a statement from you. Shouldn't take too long. 'Kay?"

McFarland sucked in a deep breath and nodded again. "Yes, please. Happy to. Sure." Exhaled, loud and sloppy, eyes still locked shut.

Jordan smirked. They don't make heroes like they used to.

***

Val stirred awake, her head throbbing. Something covered her eyes—cloth of some sort, wrapped around her head. The muffled moans of a child, the kind that signaled the end of a long, unsuccessful tantrum, cut through a loud hum of highway noise. She lay on her side in a cramped space, on a hard surface, one that transferred the impact of every bump in the road to her aching temples. Her abductor had bound her hands in front of her with a zip-tie, but left her legs free. The air felt stuffy and hot. The aroma of stale sweat—her own—filled her sinuses.

After a moment, she realized her predicament. Isaac had knocked her out and shoved her in the trunk of his Porsche. How long she'd been unconscious, she couldn't even guess.

But she was alive. Jada, too, was alive—and in the car. That gave her hope.

Val worked her hands up to her face and pulled off the blindfold. Not much help—everything remained pitch black. She rolled onto her back and felt around her, discovered the glow-in-the-dark handle to the release latch. She could pop open the trunk, maybe, but then what? Jump out? Even if she survived the fall at fifty or sixty miles per hour, she'd get royally bruised up, possibly break some bones. Or the next vehicle that came along would run her over. Plus, Isaac would still have Jada, and God knows where he'd go from there. No, trying to escape that way wouldn't solve anything.

But she couldn't do nothing. Isaac wouldn't let her go—Val had seen Jada, could connect it to the car, and to him. He'd need to make Val disappear. Permanently.

For the first time, real fear gripped her, for her own safety rather than Jada's. Nobody knew where she was, or what had happened to her. Tanisha Jordan knew she'd been luring Isaac in, but what help was that now? She'd rushed in, as her uncle used to say, "where angels feared to tread," and her carelessness had cost her. It would cost her even more dearly, unless she got out of this.

But escaping also had to include rescuing Jada.

She envisioned the girl's face, remembering the picture Rhonda had shown her, made real by the quick glimpse she'd caught of her before getting knocked unconscious. And by the sound of the child's intermittent sobs that leaked through the seat between them. That image morphed against her will to that of her own 18-month-old niece, Ali, whom she loved more than life itself. Jada and Ali had never met, and probably never would. But they fused into a single identity in her mind: the face of joyous, hopeful virtue. A life just beginning, a soul too young to be subjected to the cruelty that lay ahead in Isaac's hands. She would never allow that to happen to her niece, and could not let it happen to Jada.

Val sensed the car turning and slowing to a stop. The engine remained on, but movement up front shifted the Porsche's balance, enough to notice. A metallic *click* startled her, and she realized that the trunk lid had lifted a few inches, allowing bright light and intense heat to pour in. She snagged a metal protrusion in her bound hands, preventing the trunk from opening farther. Her body shook, and she feared she might let go, but somehow, she held on.

A door slammed. Footsteps in gravel alongside the car grew louder, then stopped. Another click, this time a sound she recognized from her youth. On her tenth birthday, Uncle Val had brought her, without her parents' blessing or knowledge, to a pistol range to teach her to shoot. She identified the sound: a pistol slide being racked to load a bullet into the firing chamber. Then a second click, that of a safety being released.

She froze again, her mind racing. Should she

jump out and try to run? That seemed futile—he'd shoot her in the back. Or, should she roll to one side, in case he shot through the trunk? That struck her as unlikely, in such an expensive car— unless he planned to abandon the Porsche afterward.

She recalled the advice Uncle Val had imparted at the pistol range: when everything seems hopeless, get aggressive.

A pudgy hand gripped the bottom edge of the rear of the trunk, and the lid began to rise. Instinct kicked in, and she yanked it back down. A loud grunt preceded the sound of feet shuffling on gravel, and it sounded like her captor was leaning into the effort. The reason for its failure to open hadn't occurred to him, apparently.

That gave Val her one opportunity to seize the element of surprise, and she took it.

She let go with her hands and kicked upward with both feet. The lid shot skyward for a moment, then shuddered to a stop with a loud thud, followed by a cry of pain. Apparently the spoiler had struck Isaac in the face. He stumbled backward and the trunk sprang open.

Val rolled to her feet and leaped in a single motion toward the falling body. With her hands bound, she resorted to her next-best weapon. The crown of her head crashed into the man's forehead, her elbows pressed against his temples. They landed together on the ground with a loud *whump*, with Val on top. Sharp pain ran up her arms as her elbows crashed onto the pavement. Her forehead smashed into his, and this time she, too, absorbed some of the impact.

Her eyes dimmed, her head seemed to twirl in a

dizzying motion, and her body weighed a thousand pounds. She fought nausea, tried to sit up or roll off of him, but her arms would not move. In the back of her mind, she heard a baby cry.

Then, blackness.

\*\*\*

The world spun around her. Blackness faded into bright red light through her eyelids. Men and women shouted. Footsteps pounded. Val's head felt like someone had placed a two hundred pound barbell on it, and both arms ached. Someone touched her face—

Val's eyes shot open. Above her, a man's face. Latino. Round and tanned, with dark hair. Unfamiliar. But not angry or sinister.

A friendly face, even.

Her focus widened, and she took in more of her surroundings. She lay on a gurney, elevated a few feet above the ground. The man hovering over her wore blue scrubs and held a stethoscope to her chest. A paramedic, or a doctor or nurse. His hand fell away from her face, and she realized he'd been checking her breathing or her eyes.

The man smiled at her. "Well, that's a good sign," he said. "Can you hear me, Miss Dawes?"

Val closed her eyes again, took a deep breath. "Yes, thank you." She propped herself up on her elbows. "Where's Jada?"

"The little girl?" His smile broadened. "Safe, thanks to you."

"Is our hero awake?" said a familiar voice. Moments later, the friendly visage of Tanisha Jordan appeared. "Welcome back to the land of the living, my friend. We were worried about you."

"Still are," the paramedic said. "In a few minutes, we're sending you to the hospital. Are you in pain?"

Val nodded, which only made her head pound harder. "I have a horrible headache. Do you have any water?" She sat up all the way and accepted a bottle from another paramedic, sipping it while watching the crime scene unfold around her. Two uniformed officers tied yellow tape to trees, road signs, and shrubs to cordon off the area. Another officer examined the Porsche, its doors and trunk wide open. A man in scrubs tended to Jada in the back seat of a patrol car. A second cruiser held the slumped figure of Isaac Lewis, hands cuffed behind him.

"What happened?" she asked Jordan.

"I was about to ask you the same thing," the detective answered. "We found you lying on top of the suspect, both of you unconscious and bleeding. Don't touch that," she said when Val noticed the gauze wrapped around her head for the first time. "We figured you either beat him senseless with your forehead, or you had some amazing roadside hanky-panky." She held up a broken zip-tie, indicated the red welts on Val's wrists, and grinned.

Val glared at Jordan, vomit threatening to explode from her gut. "Ew," she said, shaking her head. "You cops have some crazy gallows humor."

"We'd better get her to the hospital," the paramedic said. "Sorry, Detective. Your interview will have to wait."

"Just one more thing." Jordan squeezed Val's shoulder. "Ms. Dawes, I just wanted to thank you. And, okay, I lied—there's a second thing." She fixed Val with a steady gaze and a slight smile. "You will make a hell of a cop someday," she said, "should you choose that route."

Val reclined back onto her elbows, her head still pounding. "If this is what it's like, Detective," she said, "let's mark me down as 'doubtful.' At least, for now." Then dizziness overcame her, her eyes closed, and she fell back to the gurney, unconscious.

# Chapter Sixteen

Isaac broke in mere minutes under what Tanisha Jordan considered light pressure. He confessed to his role in the scheme and named his co-conspirators in less than an hour. In exchange, he received a slight reduction in sentencing and the proviso that they wouldn't serve in the same prison facility. Authorities caught the Creole woman who'd posed as Rhonda's mother at the Hartford train station, and her story confirmed Isaac's.

Jordan found Rhonda in the pediatric wing of the hospital, seated next to the child's bed, both arms wrapped around the hunky Asher Mulholland. "How's Jada?" Jordan asked.

"Doctors say that Jada had missed a few meals and suffered from dehydration, but nothing serious," Asher said with a reassuring smile at Rhonda.

"Says you!" Rhonda gave his nose a playful swat. "If only she could tell us everything that happened. The poor girl must have been frightened to death the whole time. I know I was!"

Asher hugged Rhonda again, then addressed Jordan. "We should be able to take her home soon. Child Services needs to read the police report and interview the doctor. God knows what they expect to find out."

"I'll speak to Adonna Matthison," Jordan said. "And the doctors. Don't you worry about custody. I'll do everything I can to make sure things go your way."

"Thank you, Detective," Rhonda said. "So, it was Isaac who masterminded this whole thing?"

Jordan chuckled. "Hardly. Isaac was the local muscle—the errand boy of the international baby ring. He identified Jada as the target and hired the woman who pretended to be your mother, but he reported to much smarter and meaner people. It wasn't his first attempt, but it will be his last."

"And Rizzo...?"

Jordan shook her head. "Neither Isaac nor his accomplice named Rizzo, nor your brother. For now, they're in the clear."

Rhonda peeled herself out of Asher's strong arms and wrapped Jordan into a bone-crushing hug. "Thank you for saving my baby."

"I'd love to take the credit, but I can't," Jordan said. "Not much of it, anyway. Valorie Dawes is the one who found and stopped him. That girl knows how to use her head, in more ways than one."

"Please extend my thanks to her also," Rhonda said, breaking the embrace.

"Why don't you thank her yourself?" Jordan said. "I'm heading over to her room next."

Rhonda bowed her head. "I doubt she wants to speak to me right now."

"I can't imagine anyone she'd rather hear from than you," Jordan said.

Rhonda turned to Asher, who dipped his head in a curt nod. "I'll go with you."

"No." Rhonda held up her hand. "Stay with

Jada, in case she wakes up. Ms. Jordan will come with me, won't you, Detective?"

"Of course." After giving her time to hug Jada again, the detective led Rhonda out of the room and down the hall to the Urgent Care wing. As they crossed the lobby, a curly-haired man with olive skin rushed toward them.

"Rhonda!" Marty Rizzo spread his arms as if to embrace Rhonda.

Rhonda let out a frightened yip and cowered behind Jordan. "Keep him away from me!" she whispered. "Please!"

"Keep your distance, Mr. Rizzo," Jordan said. "Rhonda doesn't want you here right now."

"Where's our baby?" Rizzo said. "I have a right to see her!"

"A certain restraining order says otherwise." Jordan stretched both arms wide to block him from both Rhonda and Pediatrics.

"That's a bunch of crap," Rizzo said. "As her father, I have rights. I'll sue. I'll close this hospital if I need to!"

Jordan moved toward him. "Mr. Rizzo, please—"

"That won't be necessary." Rhonda emerged from behind Jordan and extended a hand to Rizzo. "Marty, I'm glad you're concerned about her. If you promise to be good, I'll allow you to visit with her for a few minutes."

Jordan drew in a deep breath. "Rhonda, I don't think—"

"It's all right." Rhonda faced Rizzo again. "Asher's in there. He can take care of Marty if he misbehaves."

"That boxer guy?" Rizzo backed up a step, his

skin paling. "Listen, I'm not looking for trouble. I just want to hold my little girl."

"And you may," Rhonda said. "Asher won't interfere. I'll call him and tell him to keep a watchful eye on you, but to allow you in. Five minutes."

Rizzo's shoulders fell. "Okay, okay." He took a step, then whirled back to face Rhonda again. "Listen, babe, I'm sorry about how things ended between us. Maybe you and me—maybe we can get together, try to work it out—"

"Forget it, Marty," Rhonda said. "And the clock's ticking. You're down to four and a half minutes."

Rizzo stared at her a moment, then dashed toward Pediatrics. "I haven't given up on you!" he yelled over his shoulder. "I'll never stop loving you!"

Rhonda rolled her eyes and burst into laughter. "Never stop? That man never once told me he loved me when we dated!"

"Follow your instincts on that one." Jordan stopped her outside Val's hospital room. "I'll wait outside and let you two talk first," she said.

"Okay," Rhonda said, fidgeting and tying her fingers together into knots. "If you think it's best."

Jordan rested her hand on Rhonda's shoulder. "You'll be fine. Just be honest—with her, and yourself."

Rhonda nodded, collected herself, pushed into Val's room, and shut the door behind her.

***

Val opened her eyes at the sound of the hospital room door closing and opened them wider when she saw her visitor. "Well, hello, stranger," she said. "I didn't expect to see you today. How's

Jada?"

Rhonda shuffled over to the side of Val's bed and held her hand. "Safe, thanks to you," she said. "But my little girl has cried enough to last a month."

Val grinned and sat up in the bed. Her fingers felt clammy and cold, but she swallowed her nervousness and squeezed Rhonda's hand. "I'm glad. If someone ever took Ali...I don't know how you coped during all that."

Rhonda wiped tears from her eyes. "I wouldn't have, without you."

"Ah, I don't know." But Val's eyes grew moist as well.

"Val..." Rhonda's voice trailed off. A long moment passed. "I'm sorry for how I treated you. After all you did for me...I feel awful."

Val squeezed Rhonda's hand. "You were under so much stress. I would have behaved the same, or worse, I'm sure."

"You're too kind, Val." Rhonda lifted her gaze and smiled. "I don't deserve you." Silence hovered in the air for several seconds, then Rhonda cocked her head. "I'm sorry, I haven't even asked about your injuries!"

Val laughed, and it made her head ache. "The doctors found symptoms of a concussion, so they'll hold me overnight for further observation. I'll miss Criminology class—oh, damn! I never signed up for a research topic." Her headache intensified, and she lay back down, freeing her hand from Rhonda's. "Uh...did you sign us up, or...?"

Rhonda's face grew long, her lips turned down in a sad frown. "Val, I can't be your partner on the project. I've been thinking, and—"

"I understand," Val said. She blinked away tears—where did they come from?—and closed her eyes. "Given the circumstances."

"No, no, you don't understand," Rhonda said. She took Val's hand again. "Please don't tell Asher, but... I resigned from the University today. I've decided to return to Jamaica."

Val shot upright again, redoubling the pain echoing around in her head. "Rhonda, are you positive you want to do that? Sure, this has been traumatic, but is Jamaica safer than Connecticut?"

Rhonda laughed. "Not for most people. But I grew up there, my family is there...I belong with them. Connecticut is...well, very white and middle-America, you know? Not as accepting for folk like me. And...for Jada."

Val heaved a deep sigh. "What about your education, and the opportunities for Jada's future? What about—"

"I will continue my studies there," Rhonda said. "Val, I appreciate your concern. But I know what I want to do." She squeezed Val's hand one more time. "Please respect my wishes and the thought I've put into this."

Val exhaled a noisy breath and smiled. "Sorry, I didn't mean to 'white-splain'. I guess I was just hoping...we could, you know, be friends." The tears she'd fought so hard won the battle and flowed down her cheeks. A new pain competed with the ones in her head and limbs, a hollow ache that tore at her heart and forced a lump into her throat.

"Valorie." Rhonda edged closer, her face wet with tears. "We are friends, *mon cher*. Distance cannot get in the way of that." She brushed a hair from Val's eyes, letting her hand rest on Val's cheek. "And if anyone ever kidnaps someone you love...well, my girl, I owe you one."

Val laughed, unleashing a fresh torrent of tears. She wiped them away and blushed. "Lordy. Why am I blubbering so much? Must be the pain meds making me all mopey."

"Must be," Rhonda said, grinning.

Val gazed at her a long moment. "Selfishly, I want to keep arguing, to convince you to stay. But I won't. Deep down, I want what's best—for both of you." She closed her eyes again and winced again at the pain.

"Goodbye, Valorie," Rhonda said. "I won't forget you...friend."

"I won't forget you, either," Val said. Or at least, she hoped she said it. She couldn't be sure.

When Val opened her eyes again, Rhonda was gone.

***

Val lay awake for several minutes, taking in all that had transpired over the past few days. She had embarked on a whole new adventure of starting college and living away from home. In so doing, she'd put her athletic scholarship at risk by missing one practice and arriving late to another. That she could blame on having gotten mixed up in a crazy kidnapping scheme, even getting abducted herself. A man had slugged her in the head and came within moments of killing her. Perhaps scariest of all, she'd made a new friend, something she rarely did growing up in Clayton.

And in the space of less than 48 hours, she'd already said goodbye to her new friend. She'd put herself out there emotionally, without even thinking about it, and come away with a fresh bruise on her heart.

Val had also created confusion in one area she'd thought nothing would ever shake. As a young girl, she'd committed to following in her uncle's footsteps and becoming a police officer. But fighting crime turned out to be as dangerous as everyone said. Chad, Dr. Hirsch, even Detective Jordan had warned her about that. Now, having skirted with death, it felt far more visceral and real. The pain all over her body reinforced those negative thoughts.

A knock startled her out of her self-pity. "Ms. Dawes?" Tanisha Jordan said through the door. "May I come in?"

"Please do, Detective," she called out. Or tried to. Her voice sounded so soft, she wondered if anyone heard her. But a moment later, the detective's smiling face appeared at her bedside.

"Is this where the line forms to congratulate you for capturing Mansfield's most dangerous felon?" Jordan said.

"Starts, and ends," Val said with a tired smile. "All I did was let a man follow me, then turn my back on him at the worst possible moment. How stupid was that?"

"But you beat the crap out of him with both hands tied behind your back," Jordan said. "Literally."

"In front, technically," Val said. "But, okay, when you put it like that, Detective—"

"Tanisha, please," Jordan said. "We ought to be on a first name basis by now, don't you think?"

"Sure," Val said. "Tanisha."

"Can I call you Valorie?" Tanisha asked in a soft voice.

Val nodded and smiled.

Jordan pulled the guest chair closer to the bed and sat, putting her head a foot or so from Val's. "I hope all this hasn't soured you on wanting to become a cop," she said. "Although I'd understand if it did."

"I'd be lying if I said it hadn't," Val said, her face reddening.

"It wasn't fair of me to put you in harms' way like that," Tanisha said. "Without proper backup and training—hell, we wouldn't send a seasoned officer out like that. It was a huge mistake, and I'm so sorry."

"It all happened so fast," Val said. "I guess I didn't make very good choices. Probably not the kind of decision-making you'd hope for in a cop."

"On the contrary," Tanisha said. "You did remarkably well. You have excellent instincts, Valorie, and a real tenacity about you. You're tough, quick-thinking, and smart. All qualities we seek when recruiting police officers."

Val blushed again. "Thanks. That means a lot." She paused a moment, let it sink in. "So, if I needed a letter of recommendation someday..."

"In a heartbeat." Tanisha patted her hand. "Anywhere, anytime. But I hope you'll apply to Mansfield when you're ready. Of course, I'd have to recuse myself from the hiring process."

Val frowned in puzzlement. "Why's that?"

Tanisha smiled at her. "They might consider me biased, recommending one of my friends."

Val smiled, then choked in surprise. "You think of me as your friend? A privileged white girl, half your age—"

"Hey, you calling me old?" Tanisha said in mock indignation. "That's a hell of a thing to say."

Horrified, Val fought for words. "No, I meant I'm just a kid, really—"

Tanisha burst into laughter. "Your buttons are easily pushed, aren't they?" She laughed again, then grew more serious. "I mean it, Val. I hope this isn't the last I see of you—personally or professionally."

Warmth rose in Val's chest. "I hope not, too, Tanisha."

"So," Tanisha said, "does this mean you've decided?"

Val thought for a moment. Having a female friend and a mentor to turn to made the prospect of police work seem much more attractive to her.

But that felt so clinical. She pushed her thoughts aside and listened to her heart. It spoke loud and clear, reinforcing what she'd known since grade school: her goal in life was to protect and to serve, just like her uncle Valentin.

"I *have* decided," she said, taking Tanisha's hand in hers. "When I graduate, I will return to Clayton and become a police officer."

"Not Mansfield, Valorie?" Jordan asked in a teasing tone.

"I'll keep Mansfield in mind as Plan B," Val said. "And, Tanisha? Please." She fixed the detective with a steady gaze and smiled. "My *friends* call me Val."

# From The Author

Thank you for reading *In Search of Valor*. If you enjoyed reading it, won't you please take a moment to leave me a review at your favorite retailer? And please, tell your friends!

## Questions to consider when posting a review

What made me first decide to read this book was...

As I started reading, the first thing that drew me into this book was...

What I liked most about the main character was...

What I liked most about the plot was...

What I liked most about the author's writing style was...

My favorite part of the story was...

Compared to other books in this genre, this book was...
___ Among the best ___ Better than most
___ About average ___ Not as good ___ Among the worst

I would / would not recommend this book to a friend because...

# ACKNOWLEDGMENTS

Sometimes a story idea comes to a writer from an outside source—something we might read in the news, see on TV, or chance upon in conversation. Other times, a story wakes the writer up at night and won't go away until it gets written. *In Search of Valor* is one of the latter kind, interrupting my work on what will now be the third work in this series (*A Better Part of Valor*). It seems the story of Valorie Dawes will not be told in order, at least from the writer's-desk point of view.

That being said, I kicked the idea around for this story with my usual cadre of trusted writer and reader friends, and they all responded with such enthusiasm that I knew it had to take precedence. Those people—Randal Houle, Kate Kort, and Debb Stanton—also provided significant and valuable feedback to early drafts, including rewrites, without which I would never have reached the finish line.

Patsy Silk not only provided story feedback, but also stepped up again as my editor and proofreader. I hope I fixed all the mistakes that she found. Any that I missed are my fault, not hers.

I can never give kudos enough to Steven Novak, whose creativity and patience with me once again yielded an amazing cover design.

Of course, my father, Donald Corbin, first dreamed up the basic story and main character for *A Woman of Valor*, and I loved it from the start. I wish you were still here, Dad, so you could read all of the other stories your idea inspired.

Nobody contributed more to my writing career

than my dear mother Patricia Corbin, who awakened in me the love of books and reading, and always encouraged my love of writing.

But most of all, thanks to Renée, the kindest, most patient, most beautiful person I've ever known, whose smile lights up the darkest night and brightens the sunniest day. You not only patiently read my chapters and gave me feedback, but gave me love and encouragement, without which I would simply not be able to do this. Your support makes all of this possible. I love you.

# ABOUT THE AUTHOR

Gary Corbin is a writer, actor, and playwright in Camas, WA, a suburb of Portland, OR. His creative and journalistic work has been published in *BrainstormNW*, the *Portland Tribune*, The *Oregonian*, and *Global Envision*, among others. His plays have enjoyed critical acclaim and have been produced on many Portland-area stages.

Gary is a member of the Willamette Writers Group, Nine Bridges Writers, the Northwest Editors Guild, PDX Playwrights, and the Bar Noir Writers Workshop, and participates in workshops and conferences in the Portland, Oregon area.

A homebrewer and home coffee roaster, Gary is a member of the Oregon Brew Crew and a BJCP National Beer Judge. He loves to ski, cook, and root for his beloved Patriots and Red Sox. And when that's not enough, he escapes to the Oregon coast with his sweetheart.

# Connect with Gary Corbin

Keep up to date with the latest at
http://www.garycorbinwriting.com


Follow me on Twitter:
http://twitter.com/garycorbin


Follow me on Facebook:
https://www.facebook.com/garycorbinwriting


Follow my Amazon Author Page (and review this
book!) http://smarturl.it/GaryCorbinAuthor


Favorite me at Smashwords:
https://www.smashwords.com/profile/view/Gar
yCorbin

# ALSO BY GARY CORBIN

## *Valorie Dawes Thrillers*
### A Woman of Valor

A rookie policewoman, who had been molested as a young girl, pursues a serial child molester–and struggles to control the anger his misdeeds awake in her. Can Valorie overcome the trauma she suffered as a child and stop this dangerous criminal from hurting others like her—or will her bottled-up anger lead her to take reckless risks that put the people she loves in greater danger?

*ISBN: 978-0-9974967-9-6*
*Available in hardcover, paperback, audiobook, and all eBook formats at garycorbinwriting.com, and at your favorite local retailers.*

*Check the* **free sample chapter** *from this book below!*

## A Better Part of Valor

*The exciting sequel to **A Woman of Valor***

When Valorie Dawes discovers the body of a young girl who had also been sexually molested, Lt. Gibson assigns her to assist the detectives investigating the case. Then Clayton Mayor Megan Iverson, candidate for governor of Connecticut, ties her political fortunes to the case, vaulting herself into the lead in all of the major polls with her law-and-order campaign.

Iverson's meddling in the case costs them dearly when key evidence disappears and other evidence, withheld for strategic reasons, gets leaked to the press. The pressure intensifies when a former campaign aide, Val's childhood friend Amy, becomes the next victim.

*Can Val find and stop the killer before he strikes again?*

*Expected release: Summer, 2020*

# *The Mountain Man Mysteries*
## The Mountain Man's Dog

In the small town of Clarkesville, in the heart of the Oregon Cascade Mountains, Lehigh Carter, a humble forester, stumbles into the complex world of crooked cops and power-hungry politicians...all because he rescues a stray, injured dog on the highway.

The *Mountain Man's Dog* is a briskly told crime thriller loaded with equal parts suspense, romance, and light-hearted humor, pitting honor and loyalty against ruthless ambition and runaway greed in a town too small for anyone to get away with anything.

*ISBN: 978-0-9974967-1-0*
*Available in hardcover, paperback, audiobook, and all eBook formats at garycorbinwriting.com, and at your favorite local retailers.*

## The Mountain Man's Bride

In this thrilling sequel to *The Mountain Man's Dog*, the murder of popular Acting Sheriff Jared Barkley puts Lehigh and Stacy's plans to marry on hold when Stacy is arrested for committing the crime.

But evidence of a secret affair makes even Lehigh wonder if he should fight for her freedom against the corrupt local machine that accused her.

*ISBN: 978-0-9974967-3-4*
*Available in hardcover, paperback, audiobook, and all eBook formats at garycorbinwriting.com, and at your favorite local retailers.*

## The Mountain Man's Badge

Appointed to fill out the unexpired term of disgraced sheriff Buck Summers, mountain man Lehigh Carter investigates the murder of sleazy businessman Everett Downey, murdered in a forested area frequented by off-season hunters and poachers.

As the evidence mounts, pointing to Stacy's father, George McBride, Lehigh battles the mistrust of the entire sheriff's department as well as the District Attorney, the County Commission Chair and his own wife—until he finds shocking evidence of the killer's true identity.

*ISBN: 978-0-9974967-7-2*
*Available in hardcover, paperback, and all eBook formats at*
*garycorbinwriting.com, and at your favorite local retailers.*

# Lying Injustice Thrillers
## Lying in Judgment

*A man serves on the jury trying a man for the murder that he committed!*

Peter Robertson, 33, discovers his wife is cheating on him. Following her suspected boyfriend one night, he erupts into a rage, beats him and leaves him to die...or so he thought. Soon he discovers that he has killed the wrong man—a perfect stranger.

Six months later, impaneled on a jury, he realizes that the murder being tried is the one he committed. After wrestling with his conscience, he works hard to convince the jury to acquit the accused man. But the prosecution's case is strong as the accused man had both motive and opportunity to commit the murder.

As jurors one by one declare their intention to convict, Peter's conscience eats away at him and he careens toward nervous breakdown.

*Lying in Judgment* is a courtroom thriller about a good man's search for redemption for his tragic, fatal mistake, pitted against society's search for justice.

*ISBN: 978-06926426-8-9*
*Available in hardcover, paperback, audiobook, and all eBook formats at garycorbinwriting.com, and at your favorite local retailers.*

## Lying in Vengeance

Two months after serving on the jury trying a man for the murder that he committed, Peter Robertson's worst nightmare comes to fruition: Christine, his beautiful and charming fellow juror, knows his dark secret and uses it to blackmail him.

The price of her secrecy: Peter must kill again, this time to stop Kyle, the man who torments Christine and threatens her very existence.

Their sizzling nascent romance gets interrupted when Kyle kidnaps her. Peter's daring rescue provides him the opportunity to commit the awful deed. Peter refuses, however, only to discover that his best friend Frankie may have committed the act in his place. Or was he framed?

Peter's relentless search for evidence to clear his lifelong pal forces him to confront his demons and risk his own freedom—and his life—as he battles the ruthless, manipulative, and resourceful woman who always seems one step ahead and knows his every move.

*ISBN: 978-0-9974967-5-8*
*Available in hardcover, paperback, audiobook, and all eBook formats at garycorbinwriting.com, and at your favorite local retailers.*

# A Woman of Valor

by Gary Corbin

# Chapter 1

Valorie Dawes tiptoed to her roommate's bedroom door. She could never be sure if Beth had company, or if she'd pulled an all-nighter to study for exams and wanted to sleep all day, or both. Usually, Beth left some sort of signal in their tiny common living space if she didn't want Val to disturb her before 9:00 a.m. But during finals week, none of the usual rules applied, except one: waking her meant Val would have hell to pay.

She crept closer to the door, grimacing every time the old floorboards creaked, and listened. Nothing. Maybe Beth hadn't even come home.

Val waited another moment, pressing her ear to the door. A soft buzzing sound seemed to emerge from within. Snoring, or perhaps her morning alarm. Maybe if she brought coffee—

The door swung open, and Val jerked back in a panic. The five-foot seven, pear-shaped figure of her lifelong friend appeared in the darkened doorway, her eyes bleary between tousled locks of brown hair.

"What are you doing there?" Beth asked, striding past her toward the kitchen in a pale-yellow bathrobe. "And please, tell me there's caffeine. I've still got to cram for my Business Ethics final today."

"Fresh, dark, and strong," Val said, pausing for Beth's stock reply.

"Like my men," Beth said.

Val grinned with relief. Good old Beth.

Beth poured coffee into a tall ceramic mug and made a pouty face. "I hate that you're finishing a semester early. I'll never find a roommate as good as you." She searched the fridge and dumped a pint of creamer into her mug. "Oh, thanks for getting groceries. Otherwise we'd have starved today."

"I'll be out of here by dinner," Val said, "once I drop my application in the mail. I was hoping you'd look at it for me...?" She pointed to a stapled set of printouts on the kitchen table. "After you've had your coffee, of course."

"Dammit, Val, this makes me sad. It's the end of an era." Beth poured Val a mug of black coffee and they sat opposite each other at the table. They toasted each other with their mugs and took long sips of the tasty brew.

"It's just a few months," Val said. "We'll be roomies again once we're both back in Clayton. That's still the plan, right?"

Beth's gaze floated upward, over Val's shoulder. "Good morning, gorgeous," she said.

Val furrowed her eyebrows. What a curious thing to say. She started to reply, but something moved in her peripheral vision. No, not something. Someone. She turned, and the bare, muscular chest of a large, dark-haired man filled her vision. Close to her face. Close enough to smell his cheap cologne.

*Cologne that brought her back to the worst*

*day of her life—the day a man towered over
her, dominated her, hurt her—*

Val leaped out of her chair, hooked her right foot
behind the dark-haired man's left leg, and pushed
him to the floor. She stepped over him and spun
around, crouched in a jiu jitsu fighter's stance,
fingers curled and ready to strike.

"Val! What the hell?" Beth shouted, jumping to
her feet. Her coffee had spilled all over her
bathrobe, drenching her and the floor. "Geez, Rick,
are you all right?"

Rick, who Val realized was Beth's latest
conquest, picked his tall, muscular frame off the
floor and wiped coffee off of his face. He wore only
a set of red boxer shorts and a goofy smile. "I'm
fine," he said, laughing. He glanced at Beth, then
nodded to Val. "That's quite the security team
you've got there. You must be Valorie." He opened
his arms, reaching out to hug her. Val backed
away.

"Val doesn't hug, Rick," Beth said. "Go put some
clothes on."

Rick planted a long, wet kiss on Beth's lips,
grinned at Val, and ambled back to the bedroom,
shutting the door behind him.

"I've told you a thousand times, you need to
warn me when you have guys over," Val said.
"Where'd you find this one?"

"Never mind. He's temporary. Now, let me see
this application." She picked up the stapled pages
and read while refilling her coffee. Val busied
herself with cleaning up the spill.

"It looks great," Beth said after a minute. "But
Val, are you certain you want to do this? I mean,

given what you've been through..."

"I've never wanted to do anything else," she said. "You know that."

"But why Clayton?" Beth sat down again. "With what happened to your uncle there, and to you—"

"That's why it has to be Clayton," Val said, tossing the soiled rag into the sink. "No place needs an infusion of justice more than our own hometown."

"That's what worries me." Beth set the application down on the table, careful to avoid the wet spots, and rested her chin on her hands. "It feels like—and please, don't take this the wrong way—maybe you're not seeking justice so much as revenge. For your uncle, and the whole Milt incident."

"Don't say his name," Val said, clenching her eyes shut. "And I'm fine. I've put all that behind me."

"Are you sure?" Beth stood and circled the table, placing her hand on Val's shoulder. "Val, what if your anger over your uncle's death, and for what Milt did, drives you to...I mean, what if you get into tough situations with bad guys, and, you know...it doesn't end well. For them, or for you."

Beth squeezed Val's shoulders and knelt to put her face level with Val's. "I'm afraid for what could happen to you."

"Nothing will happen to me," Val said in a voice more forceful than she'd intended. "I'm not out to punish other men for what those scumbags did to my family. I just don't want other scumbags doing it to other families, and to other thirteen-year-old girls. Or grown women. Or anyone." She locked eyes with her friend, softening her tone. "I promise.

I'll be safe."

Beth's face crumpled into a sad smile. "I know you will." She gazed into Val's eyes for another moment, then looked away.

Val sighed. She might never convince her friend of how she felt. What unsettled her was that she hadn't yet convinced herself yet, either.

***

Valorie paused outside the open doorway of Lieutenant Laurence Gibson's cramped office, a shaded-glass enclosure trimmed with dark wood and beige government-issue metal chairs, desk, and filing cabinets. Gibson's bearlike figure seemed overly large for the room, and his dark brown skin, broad nose, bulbous eyes, and untamed salt-and-pepper hair exaggerated the effect.

"Come in, Ms. Dawes."

Val shut the door. The breeze of its motion caused papers to flutter, pinned to the walls or stuck to the filing cabinets with refrigerator magnets. A quick perusal told her where Gibson preferred to get his coffee, pizza, and sub sandwiches, and, like everyone else in Clayton, Connecticut, he rooted for the Boston Red Sox and New England Patriots.

"Thank you for meeting with me, Lieutenant."

Val sat in the worn, thinly padded metal framed guest chair. Gibson's desk towered in front of her, resting on cylindrical risers to accommodate his massive frame. At five-six, one twenty-five, she felt like a kid in the principal's office, rather than a 22-year-old who graduated a semester early from the University of Connecticut.

And that simply wouldn't do.

She stood and extended her hand across the lieutenant's enormous, cluttered desk, raising it uncomfortably high above the coffee cups and pencil holders stacked along its edge.

Gibson remained engrossed in a document pulled from a manila folder. Finally, he noticed her outstretched hand and took it briefly in his.

"Very impressive credentials." Gibson peered over his pince-nez glasses. "Criminology degree from UConn, graduated *cum laude*. Outstanding entry exam. Your essay on community policing was first-rate. And you're a bit of an athlete, aren't you?"

Val allowed a tiny smile. "I ran track in high school and college. I also played soccer."

"All-Metro midfielder in high school. Starter on the ACC championship team at UConn. More track ribbons than I could fit in this office. You've proved yourself a worthy competitor, Ms. Dawes." He glanced at her again. "You're a little small for a cop, but you've stayed in good shape. You should have no trouble passing the physical."

"Thank you, sir." Val blushed and held her breath. She should say more, but what? She had no idea. She kept her mouth shut.

He flipped through her application. "Have you ever shot a gun?"

She nodded. "My...uncle taught me." Dammit. She hadn't wanted his name to come up in this interview. But she smiled at the memory. Uncle Val's gift of firearms training for her tenth birthday had infuriated her parents, but only endeared him to her more.

Gibson set the application on his desk and

removed his glasses. "I'll come straight to the point. The name Val Dawes carries a certain amount of, shall we say, *respect* around here."

Val sat upright and rigid in her chair. "I'm not trading on my uncle's repu—"

"You'd be crazy not to." Gibson sat back in his chair. "Valentin Dawes was a good man and a great cop. One of the best. Some of that must have rubbed off on you."

Val's face darkened, and she stared down at her hands. "I want to be considered on my own merits, sir. On my credentials, not his."

"We wouldn't have it any other way." Gibson put his glasses on and picked up her application again. "Your exam was among the best I've ever seen. Clearly you've prepared for this for some time."

"It's all I've ever wanted to do, sir. Since I was a child."

"Since your uncle—"

"Before that."

Gibson's eyes widened, and he gazed at her a moment. Val sat motionless in her chair, torn between regret over interrupting him and relief over derailing discussion of an emotional subject. Finally, Gibson gave her a closed-mouth smile and a curt nod. Good. He understood.

"As you may know," he said, "we're on a push to recruit more women and minority officers."

She shifted in her chair, and it scraped the floor with a harsh, raspy noise. "I don't want to be an affirmative-action hire. If I don't out-compete the men—"

"You do. Don't worry. That's not the point." Gibson pushed his glasses over the bridge of his nose. "Ms. Dawes, we have 335 sworn officers in the Clayton Police Department. Guess how many are female."

She shook her head. "Twenty percent?"

"Ha! I wish." He exhaled, the wind whistling through his teeth. "Less than thirty. Not percent. *Total.* That's even worse than the national average, which is pitiful." He sighed. "People say that police work is a man's game, Dawes. It attracts people who are a little more aggressive, controlling, and confident in their physical abilities. More often than not, those people are men. And a lot of men around here want to keep it that way."

"Do you?" The words escaped before she could stop them. "Um, I mean, do you, *sir?*"

"If I did, you wouldn't be here." He leaned back in his chair. "Unfortunately, the Neanderthals outnumber the ones who agree with me. And they can make life tough on a young woman, even one with your qualifications. But given your uncle's legacy—well, let's just say I'm hoping that slows them down a little."

"So, are you saying...?"

Gibson smiled. "We'd like you to start at the academy on the first of next month. Can you do that?"

Val's heart pounded, and she could not suppress a grin. "Yes, sir!"

"Very well." He stood and offered his hand. "Welcome to the Clayton, Connecticut Police Department, Officer Cadet Dawes."